BOOK BOYFRIEND

BOOK BOYFRIENDS BOOK 1

CLAIRE KINGSLEY

Always Have LLC

Published by Always Have, LLC

Edited by Elayne Morgan of Serenity Editing Services

Cover by Cassy Roop of Pink Ink Designs

ISBN: 9781544902296

www.clairekingsleybooks.com

❀ Created with Vellum

To David, for random ideas that are magic.

To Tammi, for reminding me that I can.

And to Nikki, for helping me along the way.

ABOUT THIS BOOK

He's too hot for words.

Mia

Alex Lawson might as well be the hottest book boyfriend imaginable. A fun, romantic, possessive, panty-melting man. And the best part? He's real.

For a girl like me—a slightly awkward book addict—Alex is a dream come true, straight off the pages of my favorite romance novels.

But our story is turning into a whirlwind romance—the kind that only exists in books. Are we heading toward our own happily ever after? Or is he too good to be true?

Alex

Here's the thing. I'm not a bad guy. Lying to Mia wasn't part of the plan.

Finding success as a romance author using a female pen name wasn't part of the plan either. But sometimes life takes unexpected turns.

Like realizing the woman you're falling for is your alter-ego's online best friend.

Online, she thinks I'm a woman named Lexi. In person, she knows I'm all man. I want to worship her body and claim every inch of her.

But if she discovers my secret, I could lose everything.

1

ALEX

Sometimes in life we all have moments when we realize we screwed up so badly, there's no way out.

I'm having one of those moments.

Mia is staring at me, wide-eyed, like I just told her I murdered her mother. I didn't, for the record. But the book she's holding falls from her limp hand, and her mouth moves like she's trying to find something to say. The depth of the trouble I'm in is starting to hit me.

This is going to be bad.

"Are you serious?" she asks. "You aren't serious. How? No. You can't be."

"I am." Damn it, this is not how I wanted to tell her. "I'm so sorry. I've been planning on telling you. I wanted to tell you. It just never seemed like the right time, and when it did seem right, things kept happening."

She looks at the floor, her head slowly shaking from side to side. I'm panicking, trying to come up with the right thing to say. Is there a right thing to say when you've been lying to the woman you're in love with? If there is, I don't know what it is.

"Oh my god," she says, stepping away from me. "*Oh my god.*

I've been... and you were... this whole time... and it was... Lexi was you?"

"Yes, Lexi was me."

"Holy shit." She puts her hand on her stomach, like she might vomit. "I've been telling you things—things about you. And you've been using that, haven't you? You've been manipulating me this whole time."

"No," I say, putting up a hand. "No, Mia, I swear it wasn't like that."

"How can you say that?" she asks. "Oh god, it started in the bookstore. *Can I buy you books?* I told Lexi I wished a guy would do that, and you used it on me. You picked me up with my own line."

"No. God, Mia, I didn't know who you were then. I just thought you were cute and it seemed like a good idea."

"When did you know?" she asks, finally looking me in the eyes.

I stare at her, suddenly unable to speak. All my logic, all the decisions that seemed perfectly reasonable up until this moment come crashing down around me. The proverbial house of cards.

I really fucked this up.

"Alex, when did you find out who I was?"

"After we had dinner at Lift," I say, reluctantly. "You messaged Lexi and talked about your date. I knew it had to be me."

She gapes at me, her mouth dropping open, her eyes widening.

Yep. I'm screwed.

"How could you keep this from me?"

"The only person who knows is my sister," I say. "I kept it a secret from everybody else."

"Yeah? Well, you aren't sleeping with everybody else," she says.

I wince. "Mia, please. I didn't mean to lie to you."

"Of course you meant to," she says. "Lying doesn't happen by accident."

"No, but I wanted to tell you," I say. "I swear, I was going to."

She meets my eyes and crosses her arms. "But you didn't. Why?"

OKAY, maybe I should back up and explain why I'm standing in front of the love of my life, trying to make her understand how I'm also a woman named Lexi Logan.

Confused?

Yeah, me too.

It all started a little over a year ago. I know, that's a big jump, and you want to get to the good stuff. The *boy meets girl, they fall in love, have hot monkey sex, are pulled apart by conflict, and come back together for a brilliant happily-ever-after* stuff. Believe me, I'm all too familiar with that story.

In fact, I write them for a living.

A year ago, that wasn't me. Five days a week, I was schlepping off to my job, sitting in a dull gray cubicle, staring at a screen, writing computer code. I had a shitty uncomfortable chair, a boss who needed a throat punch, and a bunch of coworkers who were stuck in just as deep a rut as I was.

But in my spare time, I was writing a science fiction novel. I spent hours doing research, taking notes, drawing sketches. I would work late into the night, plodding away, word after word. The book kept getting longer, but I figured I would deal with that when I started revisions. Or maybe make it a trilogy. I certainly had enough material. More often than not, the sun would be staining the sky with color, and my eyes dry and gritty, before I'd finally fall into bed for a couple hours.

Only to get up and go to my shitty job.

To be fair, the sleep deprivation was probably not helping my attitude toward work.

I'd wanted to be a novelist ever since I was a kid. I almost majored in English, but my dad, ever a practical man, talked me into getting a computer science degree in case the writing thing didn't work out. The problem is, that *practical* degree led to a *practical* career, which led to the soul-sucking existence I was wallowing in.

I didn't see a way out. My job sucked. I was divorced, after a very brief and tumultuous marriage. My relationship status was basically *I love women but I'm not interested in commitment.* All I had was my writing.

But as much as I enjoyed the process, I knew deep down that it was more of a hobby than a career, at least the way I was doing it. Even if the finished product—if I ever finished it—turned out to be the best sci-fi epic ever written, it would take a stroke of luck to get it published and make enough money to quit my job. And considering I'd been working on it for years already, with no end in sight, it didn't seem like I was going to write my way to a better life.

Until my sister, Kendra, said something that altered the course of my life forever.

2

ALEX

"You know, it's too bad you're not writing something with wider appeal," Kendra says. She pushes a manila envelope across the table toward me. "Or something you could finish faster. You're such a good writer, but this is so niche."

"I didn't give it to you for marketing advice." I pour some cream into my coffee and stir. "I wanted to see what you thought about where the story is going."

A waitress sets Kendra's latte in front of her. She brings it up to her nose and smells it. "Mm, so good. I love the coffee here."

I'm having lunch with my sister at Café Presse, a little French café on Capitol Hill. I meet Kendra most Saturdays lately, and she's been giving me feedback on my novel. She's an editor, so she knows her stuff.

"You're meandering again," she says. "Up through chapter ten is really good, but then you go off on a tangent in chapter eleven and I don't know why it's relevant."

"It's relevant later," I say. "The story comes back around to it. Trust me."

She rolls her eyes. "Tell that to someone reading this.

They're going to get to chapter eleven and think, *what the fuck is this about*, and close the book. You aren't going to be there to say, *trust me*."

I rub the stubble on my chin and stare at the folder. She's probably right. She usually is. "Okay, fair enough. I'll go back through chapter eleven. Maybe I need a few more hints back in chapter seven."

"That might help," she says.

A good-looking blonde walks toward our table. I look past Kendra and catch her eye, lifting one corner of my mouth in a smile. She smiles back, but glances away and keeps walking.

Kendra lifts an eyebrow. "You are such a guy."

"What?"

"Should I take your semi-aggressive eye contact with the cute girl to mean you aren't seeing... what's her name?"

"Brandy?" I ask.

"That's it. Brandy."

"No, I'm not seeing her anymore."

"Why not?" she asks. "I thought she actually made it past your five-date thing."

"What five-date thing?"

Kendra shrugs. "Maybe it isn't *five*. I don't literally keep track of how many times you go out with someone. I just mean you don't seem to stay with anyone past about four or five dates."

She's probably right. I haven't been interested in anything more than short flings with women since my divorce.

"Why do you care?"

"Because you're my brother," she says, as if that explains life, the universe, and everything.

I take a sip of my coffee. "I broke things off with Brandy a couple of weeks ago. And before you ask, no, I'm not seeing anyone else right now."

"Don't get touchy about it," she says. "It would just be nice to see you with someone you're serious about. Someone you might actually introduce to your family."

"I'm in no hurry for that," I say. "And I don't want to talk to you about women. It's weird."

"It's only weird because you make it weird," she says.

"You really want me to start sharing the details of my sex life with you?"

"God, no," she says, rolling her eyes. "That's what I mean, I wasn't talking about sex. *You* made it weird."

The waiter brings our lunches and we start eating. This place serves amazing sandwiches. But Kendra seems distracted by something behind me.

"What are you looking at?" I ask after she looks past me for at least the tenth time.

"Nothing."

"Obviously it's something. You keep doing that." I look over my shoulder and see a couple sitting next to each other at a small table. The woman's face is hidden by the man she's with; he's kissing her, his hand on her chin. I turn back to Kendra and shrug. "It's a French café. Maybe they're caught up in the ambiance. Just ignore them."

"Yeah, but…" She looks again. "Isn't that Janine?"

I freeze. I haven't seen my ex-wife since our divorce was finalized. Seattle is a big enough city; it hasn't taken much effort to avoid her. I peek over my shoulder again. The man pulls away and I get a glimpse of her face. Yep. It's Janine.

That puts a damper on lunch. I turn back around, hoping she didn't see me.

"I'm amazed she's letting someone do that to her in public," I say. Janine was never one for outward displays of affection, especially when she was wearing lipstick. Which was always.

Kendra takes a deep breath. "Sorry. I noticed her a while ago and I was worried it would bother you."

It does bother me, but I don't want Kendra to know that. It isn't that I wish it was me obscenely making out with Janine in a public place. I don't miss being married to her. Our honeymoon period was very brief, and once the initial charm wore off, I realized I'd married someone who was demanding and judgmental. Whoever that guy is, he's welcome to her, and good luck. But there's something shitty about seeing my ex—who has clearly moved on—when I recently ended another short relationship that didn't go anywhere. And here I am, having lunch with my *sister*.

"It's fine," I say.

Kendra gives me one of her infuriating looks of sympathy. "It's okay to admit if you're lonely, Alex."

"I'm not lonely," I say. *Liar.*

She arches her eyebrow again, like she can see right through me.

"Quit doing that," I say. "Not everyone is meant to find their true love or whatever. It's not that big of a deal. And that isn't where my head is right now. There's all the stuff with Dad, and work is... work. Busy. Shitty."

"You should quit that damn job," she says.

"Right, I should stop paying rent?" I ask. "Plus, what would Dad do? You know he'd lose the house."

My dad has been struggling financially since he hurt his back. He's been out of work for several years, and the medical bills keep piling up. Even Kendra doesn't know the full extent of it, and neither does our brother, Caleb. He's busy enough getting through medical school while raising a daughter on his own, so Kendra and I are doing our best to handle things. I've been helping Dad as much as I can, but he's going to need at least one more surgery. Losing the house is just one thing on his long list of concerns.

"You should do something else," she says. "You know, you're such a good writer. That's what you should be doing."

"Well, I'm working on that part, but it takes time," I say.

"Alex, I love you, but you've been writing this book for what, five years? Somehow I don't think this is going to be a career changer for you."

I want to argue with her, but I know she's right. I love what I'm writing, but it's more of a hobby than anything else. "I know. You have a point."

"Like I said, it's too bad you aren't writing something with a wider audience," she says. "Or at least something that won't take you ten years to write."

"I don't know what else I'd write," I say.

"Do you want me to put my feelers out and see if there are any copywriter positions around?"

I shake my head. "No, I don't think I'd be any good at it. Writing what other people tell me to write would take the joy out of it."

"It might not be that bad," she says. "You could be using this talent to support yourself, instead of dying a little inside every morning when you step into your cubicle."

"Who says I'm dying a little inside?"

She raises her eyebrow at me again.

Yeah, she's right. I am dying a little inside.

"It's too bad you don't write romance," Kendra says with a wink. "We are voracious readers. Good romance authors can make a killing."

I laugh so hard I almost snort. "Yeah, I don't think so."

"Oh, I know," she says. "I'm just saying it's too bad. Seriously, I know some women who read a book a day."

"A book a day?" I ask. "How is that even possible?"

"They tend to be quicker reads. They're fun escapes. And romance readers can't get enough of them."

I shake my head. "Impressive, but I don't think that's the answer either. Thanks for trying, though."

The conversation turns to other things for a while as we finish our coffee and lunch. Someone upstairs must be looking out for me, because before we're done, Janine leaves without seeing me.

Kendra says she has errands to run, so we say goodbye outside. I walk up the hill to where I parked, and the things my sister said bounce around in my head. *What if you write something more marketable, with a bigger audience. Something you could write faster. Voracious readers. A book a day.*

I shake my head, like I can dislodge the crazy. I can't believe I'm even having this thought. Romance? I couldn't write romance. My own track record in that department isn't exactly stellar. But still, it's fiction. Could I write about people falling in love?

I'm kind of embarrassed that I'm even considering this. Kendra reads tons of romance novels, and she's one of the smartest women I know, so I don't have any kind of bias against them. It's just not my thing. Writing something so outside my genre wouldn't be any different than being a copywriter for some company. Would it?

I get in my car, wondering what the hell I'm thinking.

3

ALEX

I stare at the screen, hardly able to believe what I'm seeing. Did I actually just type that?

THE END

In all the years I've been writing—which is a lot, considering my current project is not the first book I've attempted to write—I have never, ever typed those words. I've never finished a book.

But I just finished this one.

I run a hand through my rumpled hair and blink at the screen a few times. My eyes are dry and my stubble is a full-on beard. That's no surprise, considering it's three in the morning and I've spent the last two weeks on a creative bender. I even took vacation time when I realized I had to get this story out. I've been writing from morning until well into the night for days on end. I've never been this caught up in a book before—never had the experience of my hands flying across the keyboard for hours. Usually, writing is slow and methodical for me. I consider my word choices, refer to my notes, take my time.

This book has been a completely different experience. Once I started, I was consumed by it. I couldn't stop.

I'm not sure what it says about me that this book is a full-fledged romance novel.

What Kendra said to me at lunch that day stuck in my brain like a splinter. I started thinking about writing in a different light. What if she was right? What if I had a skill—a talent, even—that I could use to make a living?

I dove into research mode. That's how I roll. I researched the shit out of publishing, book sales, marketing, everything. I learned that a huge portion of the book market is dominated by romance—especially the ebook market. Suddenly Kendra's off-hand, facetious suggestion that I write romance didn't seem so crazy. In fact, it seemed like it might be a great idea.

If I could write a decent romance novel. And that was a very big *if*.

The problem is, romance novels operate under one very specific rule: They end with a happily ever after. And as far as I'm concerned, that's a fantasy. Happily ever afters exist so rarely in real life, they might as well be unicorns.

But the idea was still intriguing, so I started reading some popular romance novels. And when I was about halfway through the fifth one (in five days, no less), it hit me: I understood these stories. They *are* a fantasy. That's the entire point. I realized I could see the underlying patterns, like lines of computer code. They made perfect sense to me. What's in these books doesn't have to exist in the real world. It's the fantasy these readers come for.

It was a startling realization, that romance novels were something I understood as well as the computer programs I'd spent years writing.

With all that material still buzzing in my mind, I decided to throw caution to the wind and see if I could write my own. I spent a day taking notes and coming up with characters and a plot. I took what I knew about the books I'd read—what made them work—and sketched out an outline. I made sure it would hit the same notes that readers seemed to love.

Then in a two-week caffeine-fueled haze, I wrote.

I gaze at those two little words again, then hit save, back up the file, and turn off my laptop, wondering what the hell I'm doing with my life.

KENDRA PLOPS DOWN into the chair across from me, her eyes wide. "Are you fucking serious?"

"Am I serious about what?"

She pulls the manuscript of my romance novel out of her bag and sets it on the table. "This."

"It can't be that bad," I say.

"That *bad*?" she asks. "Are you kidding me right now?"

I have the sinking feeling that I just wasted two weeks of my life. Damn it, I actually thought this thing had potential. "Kendra, you're going to have to be more specific. Lay it on me. I can take it. How awful is it?"

"Alex, this is one of the best books I've ever read in my entire life."

My brow furrows and I open my mouth, but I don't say anything for a second. Is she messing with me? "What?"

"This book is incredible," she says. "It has absolutely everything a good romance should have. Fun and interesting characters. A hero who's a dream. So much emotion. Flaming hot sex. I was so caught up in the story, I forgot to be weirded out by the fact that *my brother* wrote all that naughty stuff. The ending is spectacular. I laughed. I cried. I wanted to throw it across the room, but at just the right parts. And the ending... oh my god. Did you really write this?"

"Yeah, I did."

"When?"

"Over the last couple weeks," I say. "I gave it a once-over after I finished it, but I'm sure it's full of errors. Mostly I just wrote it, printed it, and gave it to you. I didn't want to spend more time on it if it wasn't any good."

She looks at me like she's never seen me before, shaking her head slowly. "I can't believe you wrote this."

"Um, thanks? I guess?"

"I just didn't know you had this kind of thing in you," she says. "I'm being completely honest with you right now. This is an amazing novel. It needs an edit, but it's not even that bad. Your writing is very clean, if this is basically a first draft. You *nailed* this. In every sense of the word."

"Wow, I didn't expect this big of a reaction," I say.

"You need to publish it."

I rub my jaw and glance away. That's the idea, of course. I didn't just write a romance novel for the fun of it (although can I admit that it *was* fun?). But I'm still not sure about the whole thing.

"I don't know. This feels so rushed. I just wrote it. And publishing is a completely different thing than writing a book. I wouldn't know where to start."

She arches an eyebrow at me. "Bullshit."

"What?"

"Tell me you haven't already researched everything there is to know about publishing."

"Fine," I say. "I have. But like you said, it needs an edit. And it'll need a cover, and some kind of launch plan, and—"

"I'll do the editing," she says. "It won't even take me very long."

"Okay..."

"Will you publish under a pen name?" she asks.

I raise an eyebrow. "What do you think?"

"That's smart anyway. It will sell better if people think you're a woman." Kendra sits back and chews on her lower lip. "What should we call her? Amanda? No. Desiree? No. Felicity? No, that's not it."

"What about Dixie Normous?"

"Stop," she says, although she does laugh. "Let's do a play on Alex. Alexa? No, too similar. I know, Lexi!"

"Lexi?"

"Yeah. Lexi Lawson sounds really good, but that's too close to your real name. I like the alliteration, though. Lexi... Lewis? No. Lawrence? No." She snaps her fingers. "I've got it. Logan. Lexi Logan."

"That's... okay, that's not bad," I say. "I can live with Lexi Logan. Although this is officially the weirdest conversation you and I have ever had. Are we really doing this?"

"Of course we are," she says. "Well, you are. But I'll help. Send me the manuscript in Word and I'll work on edits. You get things set up so you can publish. I'm not kidding, Alex, the book is amazing. Get it out there, get some eyes on it, and you have no idea what might happen. This is the real deal."

I take a deep breath. "Okay. Let's do this."

"And Alex?"

"Yeah?"

"Get to work on the next one."

"Wait—next one?" I ask.

"If this book is as popular as I think it's going to be, readers are going to be clamoring for another. Pick a side character from this one." She points at me. "Mark, the brother. He's perfect. We'll sexy him up a little in this book and everyone will be dying for his story. Trust me."

. . .

A YEAR LATER, I had seven novels published as Lexi Logan. The books were selling like crazy, fan emails were pouring in, and I'd quit my shitty programming job. I was working on digging my dad out of debt and making sure he got the medical care he needed. Although I was still vaguely discontent at being single, it wasn't too hard to convince myself that the rest of my life was good enough to make up for it.

You might think that's about the time I say *and the rest is history*. But really, it was just the beginning.

4
MIA

*N*ot for the first time this evening, I wonder if I should take off the scarf. It's freezing outside, and I'm close enough to the door that the scarf is keeping me comfortably warm. But my blind date is supposed to look for the girl with a blue scarf, and I'm not sure I want to go through with this.

Normally, I refuse blind dates, so they never get to the point where I'm sitting in a restaurant, nervously awaiting the arrival of a stranger. Do these things ever turn out well? In my experience, blind dates are usually uncomfortable at best, awful at worst.

The only—and I mean *only*—reason I agreed to this date was to shut up my older sister, Shelby. I haven't dated anyone in a while—blind or otherwise—and Shelby has been on my case something fierce. She got married young, and ever since she got back from her honeymoon, she's made it her mission to get me married off too.

So when Danielle, one of my coworkers, started trying to set me up with her cousin, Shelby's voice rattled around in my head

—you're going to wind up old and alone with no one but your cats for company.

I only have one cat, thank you very much. And as for winding up alone, being single past the age of twenty-one doesn't mean I'm destined to be a crazy cat lady.

Danielle showed me a picture of her cousin on Facebook, and I had to concede, he's good-looking. There was one of him dressed up in a suit at someone's wedding. I'm a sucker for a sexy man in a suit.

Okay, so maybe appeasing Shelby isn't the *only* reason I agreed to this date. It feels like it's been an eternity since I've had anything between my legs that had a pulse. And looking back, I'm not entirely convinced the last guy did.

So, while I didn't wear the *special* underwear—you know what I'm talking about—my bra and panties *do* match, and I shaved my legs. A girl should at least be prepared.

I adjust my glasses and glance at the Kindle sticking out of my purse. The temptation to get it out and read for a few minutes before my date shows up is strong. Everyone knows I'm a bookworm. Book addict, more like. I read all the time. It isn't exactly a social pastime—something Shelby reminds me of regularly—but I'm an introvert. It suits me.

The truth is, I'm more than an introvert. I'm kind of awkward around other humans. I'm a little shy, particularly with people I don't know. I spend so much time worrying about what to say and how to make a good impression, it's like my body and brain disconnect.

Which makes dating—especially a blind date with a total stranger—a special kind of torture.

But if I live through this date, I can at least tell Shelby that I gave it a shot, and maybe she'll pipe down about the dating thing for a while. And if by some miracle it works out, well, that wouldn't be terrible, now would it?

The restaurant door opens and my heart beats a little faster. It's an elderly couple—definitely not my date. I arrived early so I wouldn't have to be the one looking around at all the tables, trying to find the guy in the green shirt. It seemed much less intimidating to sit in one place and watch the door. But that also means I've already been here for ten minutes, and the extra waiting is doing nothing to calm my frazzled nerves.

The door opens again, and it's him. I recognize him from his picture, and he's wearing the green shirt he told me he'd wear.

In person, he *is* attractive. Short blond hair, blue eyes. He scans the room for a second or two before he sees me. I wave—probably with too much gusto—and he comes over to my table.

"Hi." He holds out a hand. "I'm Jeff."

I'm halfway to standing—why, I'm not sure. Standing seemed like the thing to do, so his outstretched hand takes me by surprise. I freeze, partially bent at the waist, in an almost-standing, not-quite-sitting position. Should I stand up at this point? Sit back down? I have no idea, so I take his hand and shake.

"I'm Mia," I say. He lets go and I lower myself back down into my chair. "It's nice to meet you."

"You too." He takes the seat across from me. "So..."

There's an uncomfortable pause. Oh, great. Is he as bad at making small talk as I am? I give it a shot with a question. "So you're Danielle's cousin?"

"Yep," he says. "She tells me you guys work together."

"We do." Okay, we've established something we both already knew. I need to think of something else to say—quick—but I'm not sure what to do with my hands. They're in my lap, but that feels overly proper. I set them on the table, but there's no way that looks natural. God, what am I doing?

A waiter shows up to take our drink orders. He looks at me

with his eyebrows raised, but Jeff pipes up first, ordering a vodka, straight up.

I waffle for a few seconds, wondering if I want a drink at all, but decide on a glass of pinot noir. Maybe a little wine will help me chill out and stop messing with my hand position.

"A wine drinker," Jeff says after the waiter leaves. "Fancy."

I shrug. "I guess. It's just what I usually order if I'm having a drink with dinner."

"I think you can tell a lot about a person based on their drink of choice," he says.

Am I really about to have a conversation about personality predictions based on drink orders with a man who asked for straight liquor with his dinner? And *vodka*, at that? Because it makes me think he might have a drinking problem, or he's too pansy for whiskey.

"Really?" I ask. "What does my drink say about me?"

"You want to look sophisticated." He gestures toward me. "Maybe to make up for the casual outfit."

I glance down. I'm wearing a white t-shirt and tan cardigan with my blue infinity scarf, and a pair of dark jeans with ankle boots. I *am* dressed casually, but this is a blind date at a restaurant that isn't exactly upscale. It's not like I'd wear a little black dress and pearls.

"That doesn't... I don't..." I pause, trying to figure out how to even respond to that. "Okay, what does your vodka say about you?"

He grins. "I know what I like."

Oh boy.

The waiter brings our drinks and I'm tempted to guzzle my wine. But I do have to drive myself home. We order dinner; I opt for chicken and risotto, and Jeff orders the most expensive steak on the menu. Interesting.

We chat while we wait for our food. My hands and feet chill

out and I no longer feel like I'm in danger of knocking the table over if I move. Jeff talks about his job; he works for a start-up app development company. My job isn't too interesting; I work in the business office of a hospital. We manage to keep a laid-back conversation going until our dinner arrives.

The food is good, and so far this date hasn't been a *complete* disaster. Once my initial uneasiness wears off, I relax. Jeff seems nice. He smiles at me and asks questions, like he's interested in what I have to say. I might not be great at small talk, but he starts filling in the lulls in the conversation. I sip my wine and consider ordering another; maybe we'll be here long enough that I can have two. Now that we're well into dinner, this isn't bad.

"So, Danielle tells me you like to read a lot," Jeff says.

"I do. It's one of my favorite pastimes. What about you?"

"Yeah, I read classics mostly. Dumas, Dickens, Melville, that kind of thing. I've read *Moby Dick* several times, actually."

I get the feeling he loves telling people that, like it's some kind of badge of honor. "That's interesting. I read a lot of things. I've read some of the classics too, but I prefer authors like Jane Austin and Emily Bronte. When it comes to modern novels, my favorite is romance."

He raises his eyebrows. "Romance? Huh."

Of course he scoffs. Whatever; I'm used to it, especially from people who claim to have read *Moby Dick* several times. "Yes, well, I know what I like."

"Sure," he says with a dismissive wave of his hand. "I guess I thought..."

I adjust my glasses. "You thought what?"

"I don't know, Danielle made it sound like you were a serious reader. Like we might have that in common."

My eyes widen and my mouth drops open. I reach for my wine glass, but somehow miss and knock it over. There isn't much left, but a bit of it stains the tablecloth. I watch the splotch of deep red grow as the wine spreads through the fabric. I'm torn between feeling embarrassed that I did that, and irritated at what he said.

My mouth gets ahead of my brain, and before I can decide if I want to defuse this or not, I start talking. There's no mistaking the irritation in my tone. "You think because I read romance I'm not a *serious reader*?"

"Hey, don't be offended. I just mean there are people who read and then there are *readers*. You know?"

"No, I don't know," I say. Who does this guy think he is? "How many books did you read last month?"

His brow furrows, like he's confused by my question. "Last month? I don't know, maybe one."

"I read twenty-six," I say. "That was a light month for me because work kept me busier than usual."

"You read almost thirty books in a *month*?" he asks.

"I average a book a day," I say. "I've probably read more books this year than you've read in your entire life. And yes, I've read *Moby Dick*. It was boring. I've also read *Pilgrim's Progress*, *The Scarlet Letter*, *The Great Gatsby*, *Dangerous Liaisons*, *Franken-stein*, *Vanity Fair*... should I go on? And none of them were assigned reading either. So maybe before you jump to conclusions about what someone's reading preferences—or drink choices—say about them, you should actually take the time to get to know them first."

He stares at me with a furrowed brow and carefully picks up my wineglass, setting it upright. "Wow, okay, sorry." It's clear he thinks my irritation is completely unreasonable.

Awkward Mia strikes again. I probably could have handled that better. I doubt he meant to be a dick about it. He has his opinion, I have mine, no big deal. But of course my mouth ran ahead of my brain. And of course I spilled wine. Have I ever been on a date and *not* spilled something? Certainly not a first date. No wonder I don't get many requests for a second one.

"No, it's not... I mean... I didn't..." I stop because my tongue feels all tangled. "I guess we just like different things."

The conversation is decidedly less laid-back as we finish our meal. When our check comes, I offer to pay for my dinner. But when I try to get my wallet out of my purse, I knock my napkin and fork onto the floor. I don't miss Jeff's eye roll. He takes the check from the waiter and hands over his credit card.

Once the bill is settled, we walk outside together. Jeff shakes my hand and gives me a perfunctory *nice to meet you*—with zero sincerity.

I let out a heavy sigh as I walk back to my car. Another shitty blind date on the books. At least it's over. I'm irritated with myself for the whole spilling-wine-and-running-my-mouth thing. The last guy I dated made fun of the books I read, so maybe I'm a little sensitive about it. But I didn't like Jeff all that much anyway. I suppose it would have been worse if I'd wanted to see him again and ran him off with my weirdness. At least this one ended with a sense of mutual disinterest.

Still, I'm disappointed. Despite my reluctance to be set up— this is definitely the last time I agree to a date with anyone Danielle suggests—I wouldn't mind meeting a good guy. I just can't seem to find where any of them are. Or if they really exist.

Maybe they don't. Maybe they're only in books.

5

MIA

I head upstairs, already feeling the draft of cold air that constantly runs through my building. It's an old brick building about halfway up Queen Anne, and what I gain in ambiance and a great neighborhood, I pay for in draftiness and things that break too often. But I love living here. The wall along one side of my apartment is exposed brick, and the landlord let me paint the rest of the walls when I moved in. It's positively adorable, although often freezing. I handle that particular problem with my piles of homemade knit blankets, courtesy of my beloved grandmother, and a space heater that Shelby insists will one day cause a fire.

With my key in the door, I open it carefully, wedging myself in the gap so my cat, Fabio, doesn't dash out. He's not usually a door dasher, but sometimes he slips through my legs and leads me on a chase down the hallway when I come home later than usual.

"Calm down, buddy," I say as Fabio winds his way around my ankles, rubbing his orange fur against my pants. "Mama's home. It's not like you're going to starve."

He shoots me a look like he doesn't believe that for a second, and if I'd been five minutes later, he very well might have died. I look at his round middle. Not in danger of starving. He lifts his tail and saunters into the kitchen, then plunks himself down and waits for me to feed him. If he could talk, I'm pretty sure he'd be admonishing his human slave for making him wait.

I take off my coat and scarf and toss them on the couch. "I'm coming, I'm coming." I fill Fabio's bowl, then make sure his water is fresh. Now that he has food, he no longer needs me, so I go largely ignored as I putter around the kitchen and get some tea brewing. "Aren't you going to ask about my date? No? That's probably a good thing."

I slip into the bedroom. It's only separated by a curtain, but at least it's somewhat closed off from the rest of my apartment. I take off my boots and pants, but don't bother putting on anything else. I live alone, and Fabio certainly doesn't care if I walk around in my underwear. I pull off my bra, slipping it through my shirtsleeve. Ah, now that's what I'm talking about. Nothing like taking your bra off at the end of the day.

My tea is ready, so I take my mug to the couch and sit. I already have a text from Shelby.

Shelby: How did it go? Is it over? Was it fun?

Me: It went from mildly uninteresting, to annoying, to over.

Shelby: What did you do?

I sigh and pull my green crocheted blanket over my legs. Of *course* Shelby assumes it's my fault. It's never been easy coming after perfect Shelby. She's everything I'm not. Tall and willowy, with beautiful blond hair. I'm not exactly short, but definitely not willowy, and my thick, dark brown hair is in a constant state of almost-messiness no matter what I do. Shelby was a competitive swimmer; my athletic talent was maxed out with games of tag in elementary school. Which I always lost. I'm convinced she took all the grace and coordination in the family, leaving me a bumbling, clumsy mess. She's outgoing and confident, and can talk to anyone. I get tongue-tied trying to order fast food in a drive-through.

Me: *Why do you assume I did anything? He was rude.*

Shelby: Well that sucks. Are you going to see him again, or no?

My sister might be perfect at everything, but she has no clue what it's like to date after college. She met her husband Daniel in her sophomore year at Stanford, and married him before they graduated. So the whole *being a single adult when you're not in school* thing? She's clueless.

Me: *That would be no.*

Shelby: Sorry, Mi. Next guy will be better. Can you still watch Alanna this weekend?

Me: *Of course. I'll be there Saturday afternoon.*

Alanna is my four-year-old niece, and she's awesome. Being an auntie kicks ass. My sister is pregnant again, so I've been helping out as much as I can. Our parents live six hours away in eastern Washington, but since Shelby lives about twenty minutes from me, I try to spend time with Alanna when I can to give Shelby a break.

It's still early, so I grab my laptop. I spend some time checking my blog. I run a romance book review blog under the pseudonym Bookworm Babe. It started out a few years ago as a silly side hobby. I read a zillion books, and I love writing reviews, so instead of just reviewing on Amazon, I started blogging. That expanded into things like author interviews and book news, and next thing I know, I'm getting hundreds of thousands of visitors every month. It's kind of insane, and I'm pretty sure if Shelby knew about it, she'd kill me. She'd call it a huge waste of time.

But Shelby does *not* know, nor does anyone else in my "real life." I keep my identity as Mia completely separate from Bookworm Babe. The anonymity affords me a lot of freedom when I interact with people. I'm a lot less awkward and shy when I communicate with people online, and a pseudonym gives me even more confidence. I can let out the girl I wish I could be in person.

It also gives me a degree of safety that, sadly, I think is necessary. I've had a few very nasty emails from authors angry about reviews I've written—some even threatening. A couple years ago, some guy actually stalked and attacked a book reviewer after she gave his book a bad review. I don't want any part of that drama.

So online, I'm Bookworm Babe, or BB for short. Despite what my sister says about romance novels (she views them with a high level of disdain), I've always loved them. There's simply nothing that beats getting lost in another version of reality. The heady rush of passion when two would-be lovers meet, the swirl of emotions in a fledgling relationship—I'm addicted to that shit. I lose sleep over great books all too often, but I can't help it. I live for the emotional rush I get when I read a great story.

There isn't much blog business for me to worry about tonight. I have a few emails, but I'll answer them tomorrow. I could write a review of the last book I read, but I was kind of underwhelmed. After tonight's lackluster date, I'm not feeling motivated to do much of anything.

My messenger app lights up. I open it and see I have a message from my friend Lexi.

Lexi: Hey BB, you around? Did you have your date tonight? How was it?

Me: Honestly? Not great. Could have been worse, I guess, but that's the best thing I can say about it.

Lexi: Damn. That sucks. Wanna talk about it?

Me: Not much to say. He wasn't all that, and there definitely won't be a second date. Maybe I'm too spoiled by all my book boyfriends—especially the ones you write. Real men just don't cut it.

Lexi Logan is a romance author I met through my blog. She

and I have become really good friends over the last year. We chat pretty much every day, and I'd told her how much I was dreading this blind date.

Lexi: Well, maybe I can make your night a little better.

Me: Ooh, tell me! Is the new book ready?

Lexi: It is, but only for you. The rest of the advance copies don't go out for a couple days. But since your date sucked, how about I send it to you early?

Me: Squee! Yes, please!

Lexi: It will be on your Kindle in a few. Hope you enjoy it!

Me: I always do, Lex. Thanks!

Fabio comes over and curls up near my feet. I grab my Kindle off the coffee table and unplug it, earning a squinty-eyed glare from Mr. Asshole Cat.

"What? It's not that late. And I don't have to finish the whole thing tonight. I know I have to work in the morning."

He slow blinks at me, like he doesn't believe a word I say.

"Whatever, dickhead."

I settle into the cushions and open Lexi's new book.

DESPITE THE PROFUSION of tears running down my face, my eyes feel like dry sandpaper. I sniff hard and run a hand under my nose before adjusting my glasses. It's almost over. I read the last few pages of the epilogue and let my Kindle drop into my lap from limp fingers. All I can do is stare at the ceiling for a few minutes—through fogged-over glasses, no less.

What a ride. Lexi has a way of making her characters seem so incredibly real. I feel like I take the journey with them, living the story through their eyes. I'm swept away, every single time. And she has a special skill for ripping my heart to shreds. Somehow, she always knows exactly how to stitch it back together again, placing it gently back in my chest. I put my hand over my heart to make sure it's still beating. I'm swimming in a sea of emotions, my mind reeling, my stomach full of butterflies.

This is going to be one hell of a book hangover.

Fabio lifts his head and opens his eyes, as if to say *I told you so*.

"I know, I know." I sniff again. I should have known better than to sit down to read a Lexi Logan book without a box of Kleenex. "I'm going to bed now."

It will be a while before I can sleep. Images dance through my mind, the sheer weight of all the feelings I just waded through pressing heavily against me. It's like Lexi has direct access to my brain, and she crafts stories that are everything I could possibly want in a book.

It's like she writes them just for me.

6

ALEX

"Dad," I say, trying to keep my tone as calm as possible. "We talked about this."

"You're already doing too much," he says.

I take the stack of bills out of his mail bin and thumb through them. I've been trying to talk him into putting me on his accounts so I can pay directly, but he won't hear of it. As it is, a few times a month I have to come over and argue with him about whether or not he'll let me pay his bills. I know he doesn't have the money, and I won't let him wait until his utilities are shut off again before intervening.

There's another MRI bill among the bunch. I wonder how much that one is going to be. Fortunately, my alter ego's success allows me to take care of these things without too much concern. I'm working on catching up on his house payments, and paying off the taxes and penalties he accrued over the last few years. Since he hurt his back, he's been sinking deeper and deeper into debt. Aside from being able to quit my depressing day job, my success as Lexi Logan has given me the freedom to help dig him out of this mess, and make sure he gets the medical care he needs.

"Alex, do you even have a real job?" Dad asks. "You're a consultant. What does that mean?"

I sigh and put the envelopes in the inside pocket of my coat. "It means I consult with companies who need my expertise."

My dad doesn't know the truth about my new career. I told everyone except Kendra that I quit programming to be a consultant. It's vague enough that I don't have to field too many questions, and explains why I work from home.

I want to cut off any more protests. "Speaking of my job, I need to get back to work. But I'll stop by next week."

Dad scowls and picks up his newspaper, shifting in his new recliner. It's a motorized chair that moves to help him sit and stand. His legs are weak from the nerve damage in his spine, and the chair makes things a lot easier for him. After his surgery, we hope he'll regain some of his mobility and be able to stay on his feet for longer periods of time.

"See you later, Alex," he says.

After checking up on my dad, I head to the gym to get in a good workout, then go back to my apartment. I'm ahead of where I'd planned to be on my current work-in-progress, so I take some time to tackle emails and Lexi's social media messages.

That's one side of being a popular author that I didn't expect. I get a lot of emails. When the first one came in, shortly after I published my first Lexi novel, I thought it was Kendra playing a joke on me. But sure enough, it was from a reader. The woman had taken the time to write to tell me what she thought about the book. It was touching, actually. I didn't anticipate having that kind of an effect on people.

Now I get dozens of emails a day, not to mention the social media activity. Kendra helps me run my Facebook page, but I like to stay in the loop and post things myself too. I get a lot of good feedback from fans that way. Plus, it's fun. I've gotten to know other authors, as well as book reviewers and readers—the vast majority of them women.

Projecting a female persona felt dishonest at first, but now that I'm used to it, I like the anonymity. I've never had many female friends before. Women don't usually see me as guy-friend material. For whatever reason, they go straight to boyfriend/future husband. As Lexi, I can have casual friendships with women in a way I'd never be able to as Alex.

I scroll through my emails and answer each one. I don't have time for in-depth email conversations with every reader anymore. But I like to answer them personally. The messages I get still amaze me. Women tell me how my books helped them through a bad day, or spiced up their sex lives with their husbands. One woman even said I saved her from divorce, although how that's possible, I'm not sure. Still, I appreciate the emails and messages I get. I genuinely love my fans.

A smile crosses my face when I get to my last unread email. The subject line just says *SERIOUSLY?!?!?*

It's from my friend BB, the book blogger. I open her email.

Lexi,

I'm currently nursing the book hangover from hell. I don't know whether to thank you or curse your name to the gods of romance... and day jobs. I was up half the night, but it was worth every bleary-eyed moment. This book might be your best yet, I kid you not. I'll have a full review on the blog on launch day, so keep me posted.

~BB

Instead of replying to her email, I check to see if she's on messenger. There's the telltale green dot by her name, so I send her a message.

Me: I take it by your email you liked the book?

BB: Understatement of the century. I loved it. My boss would be pissed if he knew I'm useless today because I was up late reading. I said I was probably fighting a cold. So, thanks for making me lie to my boss.

Me: Hey, you can't blame me. I didn't make you lie.

BB: Whatever, it was worth it.

Me: Awesome. That's what I like to hear. Although sorry about the hangover. Maybe you need a bloody Mary. Or a greasy burger. That's good hangover food, right?

BB: I could go for the greasy burger right about now, hangover or not.

Not for the first time, I find myself wishing I knew who Bookworm Babe really is. She's totally anonymous online. Of course, I'm not one to judge. She thinks I'm a woman named Lexi. But she's a lot of fun and I always look forward to her messages. Out of all the women my alter-ego has become friendly with, BB is my favorite. We've become good friends, our conversations moving well beyond books. We talk about a little bit of everything.

Me: Greasy burger does sound good.

BB: You should go get one. Anyway, I gotta go. Day jobs, right?

Me: Day jobs are the pits.

BB: Tell me about it.

I don't know what BB's day job is. She's never mentioned it, and I haven't asked. If she were more open about her real identity, that would be one thing. But I can understand the desire to stay anonymous.

BB goes offline—back to the demands of her day job, I suppose. I'm mildly disappointed. I like chatting with her. She's funny as hell. I love a woman who can banter with me, and she gives as good as she gets. I wonder a lot about who she is. What she might look like. Where she lives. My mental image of her is a spunky, petite twenty-something. It would be funny to discover she's nothing like I picture—kind of like how I'm nothing like she imagines me to be.

I have one more email—an announcement from a local bookstore. Amy Aurora, a well-known romance author, is doing a book signing there. I figure maybe I'll swing by and see what it's all about. Of course, as Lexi, book signings aren't something I can do. But it would be fun to see what this kind of event is like, especially for an author I consider a peer.

It's not until Saturday, so I put a reminder on my calendar before I get back to my latest book.

7

ALEX

$\mathcal{T}$he bookstore is packed. I find a parking spot, but there's a line that goes out the door. It's almost all women, although I see a few bored-looking guys standing around. I have a feeling they're boyfriends or husbands who were dragged along. I slip past the line—I'm not planning to get a book signed, so I don't need to wait. I just want to see what this sort of event is like.

I'm no expert, but this looks like a great turnout. Of course, Amy Aurora is an extremely popular author right now. I've been reading her books for research, and I can see why her readers love them. I'd love to meet her and talk shop, but I can't do that in person without outing myself as a guy.

And that is something I absolutely cannot do.

When I started this thing, I made sure there would be no connections between my real identity and my pen name. I have too much riding on this to let my secret be found out. It's not just what it would do to my personal life—although I cringe at the thought of people I know finding out I write romance. If readers knew I was a man, I'm sure my books wouldn't sell the way they do. Sure, I need to pay my bills, but more importantly, I need to pay my dad's bills. That's been sucking away all my extra money, even considering how well I've been selling.

Maybe when things calm down with my dad's health, and I have enough put away to make sure he's taken care of long term, I can loosen my vigilance and own up to being Lexi Logan. Until then? I can't risk it.

There's a big endcap with Amy Aurora's latest novel right at the front of the store. An employee is busy restocking the display. As the women in line pass, most grab a book to be signed. This looks like a great way to move a lot of hardbacks.

I head deeper into the store and wander around for a while. I glance through the sci-fi section, and there's a book that catches my eye. *Destroyer*. It's not one I've read before, and the cover is great. I haven't worked on my sci-fi project in ages—I've been too wrapped up in writing Lexi books—but reading a good sci-fi novel sounds like a nice change of pace. I've been reading, and writing, so much romance; I need a break.

I tuck the book under my arm and walk back toward the line for the book signing. There are double doors open to a separate room where Amy is doing her thing. I lean over a little so I can see inside. She's sitting at a folding table with stacks of books on both sides of her. She smiles and nods to the reader in front of her. The reader passes her a book and she signs it with a flourish, then hands it back, and the next person in line comes forward.

As I turn to go pay for my book, I bump into someone. Books scatter across the floor and I barely manage to catch her to-go cup of coffee before it falls.

I crouch down to help her pick up her books. "I am so sorry."

She kneels in front of me, her long dark hair obscuring her face, and mumbles something I can't quite make out.

"Let me get that." I scoop up her books—she has four—and hold them out to her.

Her face lifts and I'm suddenly hit by a pair of huge blue eyes, dark rimmed glasses that are too far down her nose, and full lips parted in surprise. Just as I'm getting my wits back, I catch a whiff of her and it makes my head spin. Visions of kissing this woman flood through my brain, obscuring rational thought. I snap back to reality and realize I'm staring at her like a lunatic.

We both stand, our eyes locked, as if we're magnetized. Her mouth moves, like she might say something, but she glances down at the books I'm holding out toward her and takes them.

"Thanks."

I still have her coffee in my other hand, and my own book tucked beneath my arm. "I'm really sorry about that. I guess it's crowded in here."

"Yeah," she says. "I mean... you don't need to be sorry. I mean... it's fine."

I hold out her coffee and she tries to tuck her books beneath one arm, but they almost fall again. She rolls her eyes and mumbles something as she finally gets her books situated so she can take her coffee.

"Thanks," she says. "Sorry."

"Hey, I'm the one who ran into you. No apology necessary." The line bunches up behind me, so I lightly touch the woman on the arm and guide us both deeper into the store. "Are you here for the book signing?"

"Yes, I am. Or, I was. I mean, I already did." She closes her eyes for a second and lets out a breath. "Are you here for the signing?"

I glance back at the long line of women. "Oh, no. Just getting something new to read."

"No, I didn't think you'd be here to get a book signed," she says. "Although I guess you could be. Some of her readers must be men. Maybe some gay men read romance. I don't mean I

think you're gay. If you are, that's fine, but that's not why I said
that." She lifts her hand like she's going to cover her face, but
she's holding a coffee cup. She looks at it like she just remem-
bered it's there. "God, why do I... What I meant was, are you
here *with* someone who's here for the signing?"

I grin at her. I think she's trying to find out if I'm here with a
woman. "No, I'm here alone."

"Me too," she says.

I'm glad to hear her say that. I hold out my hand. "Alex
Lawson."

She glances at the books she's holding under one arm, and
her coffee in her other hand. It takes her a few seconds to figure
out how to free one hand so she can shake mine, and I stand
here with my hand outstretched long enough that I start to feel a
little awkward.

"Sorry," she says, finally taking my hand. "I'm Mia. Mia
Sullivan."

Her hand is delicate and soft in mine, and I squeeze it gently
before I let go. "Nice to meet you, Mia."

"You too," she says.

She meets my eyes again and those kissing visions smack me
in the head. What the fuck is that about? Yeah, she's attractive,
but I don't usually have uncontrollable daydreams about women
I just met.

Okay, so she's not just *attractive*. She's beautiful. Not in a
traditional way, but maybe that's why I can't stop staring at her.
She's dressed in a dark blue t-shirt that says *Na'mastay in Bed*, a
scarf that looks like newsprint, and a pair of jeans with holes in
the knees. Her hair is full, and a little messy, and her eyes are
gorgeous. She pushes her glasses higher up her nose and I can't
help the little smile that twitches my lips.

Don't even get me started on the way she smells. I lean
toward her, just a slight movement of my feet to bring me closer,

and I get another hint of it. She doesn't smell fake, like she's wearing a lot of perfume. It's fresh, natural. Like a warm breeze in the spring.

Shit, I've been staring at her too long. Her eyes are wide, like she's afraid I'm about to drag her to my car and toss her in the trunk.

"Sorry," she says again, as if *I* wasn't the one being creepy just now. "I'll go."

"Wait," I say as she turns, but I stop because I'm not sure what I was about to say next. All I know is that I don't want her to walk away from me. Something my friend BB said to me once crosses my mind. *If it's a thing to buy a woman a drink in a bar, why isn't it a thing to buy a woman a book in a bookstore?*

Mia looks at me with her eyebrows raised. "Yeah?"

"Can I buy your books for you?"

Her mouth opens and her eyes widen, as if I said something shocking. She looks down at the books under her arm. "Oh, um, sure. I guess so. I mean, yes, that's…" She pauses again, closing her eyes for a second and taking a deep breath. "Thank you, that's really nice."

I smile again and hold out my hand. She shifts the books again, almost dropping them, and my hand darts out to catch them before they fall.

"I've got you," I say with another laugh.

We stand together in line, Mia shifting on her feet. I watch her from the corner of my eye, trying to keep the smile off my face. I'm not sure why she's so nervous, but it's very endearing. We make it up to the cashier and I set my book down first.

"This one, please," I say to the girl behind the counter. I put Mia's books next to mine. "And these for the lady."

"Of course." The cashier rings up my purchase, bags the books separately, and passes them both to me. "Have a great day."

"Thanks, you too." I hand Mia her bag and we move out of the way so the next customer can check out. "Here you go, Mia. I hope you enjoy them."

"Thank you. This is really... well, it's very sweet."

I lightly touch her arm again to steer us around the line—which hasn't shrunk at all—as we head toward the front door. We make our way past the line and onto the sidewalk outside.

"So, thanks again." She hesitates, her eyes everywhere but on me.

I'm definitely in the driver's seat here, so if I want to make something more happen, I'm going to have to just go for it. But that's fine. I prefer it that way.

"I noticed your coffee is cold. Would you like to go next door and get another cup?"

She finally meets my eyes again. "Really?"

I laugh. This girl is something else. "No, I'm messing with you. I'm an evil mastermind and inviting you to coffee is all part of my diabolical plan."

She draws her mouth up in a little grin. "Oh, I see. You're *that* kind of guy."

"What kind?"

"The kind who buys a woman books in a bookstore and gets her hopes up, then dashes them to pieces on the sidewalk outside with false promises of hot caffeinated beverages."

"I confess," I say. "But maybe today is the day I'll be reformed. Plus, I never joke about coffee."

"It's not a joking matter."

I smile at her again. "Then we agree. Come on, I'll buy."

She smiles, and some of the tension seems to leave her body. My phone dings with a text. It's probably Kendra, but she'll have to wait for my report on the book signing. For the first time in a long time, I'm much more interested in the woman walking beside me than anything to do with books or writing.

8

MIA

*A*lex holds the door open for me, and I walk inside.

I glance up at him and look away quickly. I need to stop doing that. He's going to think I'm insane. But I'm trying to figure out how a man who looks like *that* is taking *me* out to coffee.

He's extraordinary—right off the pages of one of my favorite novels. His hair is thick and dark, and swept up from his forehead. He has deep brown eyes and an exquisite jawline covered in a light beard. And when he smiles? Kill me. His eyes get a little squinty and his lips part over those beautiful, straight teeth. His body looks fit and muscular, his clothes hanging off him the way they only do when the guy is in good shape. I can see the lines of the muscles in his arms, and I am not ashamed to say I peeked at his ass while we were waiting in line in the bookstore. This guy makes jeans look *good*.

But let's forget for a second that he's one of the most beautiful men I've ever seen in real life. Because he just bought me *books*.

How many times have I said that should be a thing? I've always said I would love to have a man approach me in a bookstore and offer to buy me something to read. It beats the old *buy her a drink in the bar* thing by a mile.

And it just happened? To *me*?

And the man looks like *that*?

I'm pretty sure I'm hallucinating, but this is so good, I'm going with it until I come back to reality.

We stand in line and Alex glances at me with a little smile on his face. My heart won't slow down. Every time he looks at me, it's like getting hit with a zing of electricity.

We get to the counter and order—latte for me, cappuccino for Alex. The place is busy, but they're well-staffed, and our drinks are ready in a couple minutes. I deposit my now-cold coffee cup in the trash and Alex hands me my fresh latte.

"There are a couple seats in the back," he says.

I nod, trying with all my might to not trip over my own feet, spill my coffee, drop my books, or otherwise humiliate myself. I'm so flustered with everything that's happened in the last fifteen minutes, I barely remember how to walk. When I make it to the small table at the back of the café without suffering any embarrassing disasters, I raise my eyes to the heavens in a silent thank you to anyone and everyone who might be listening.

Alex looks so relaxed, sitting back in his chair, one hand touching his mug. I get myself into my seat, amazingly without dropping or spilling anything, and take a deep breath. I need to get myself together.

"So, Mia," he says. "I assume the books mean you like to read. Although it occurred to me when we were standing in line that maybe you were buying those for someone else."

"No, they're for me," I say. "Actually, I've already read two of them, but sometimes I like to buy hard copies for my bookshelf when it's something I really enjoyed."

"And you got one signed," he says.

"Yes, I did. I love Amy Aurora books."

He nods. "Judging by the crowd over there, I take it she's popular."

"Very," I say. "Her books are light and fun. Not too angsty. Don't get me wrong, I love a good angsty romance. But sometimes it's nice to read something lighter in between the weighty ones."

"That makes sense. It seems like there would be a lot of emotion in romance. I can see needing a break between reading heavier novels."

I'm struck by the fact that he doesn't seem put off by what I read. I'm so used to people scoffing at me when they find out what kinds of books I love—as if reading romance means I'm not a serious reader, because it isn't *real literature*. But I don't get that vibe from him at all.

"Exactly," I say. "What about you? What are you reading?" Good god, we're having a conversation about what we're reading. I am so turned on right now.

He pulls out his book and shows me the cover. "I haven't read this author, but it looks good. I'm in the mood for something new."

"It looks great."

I relax and the worst of my klutz tendencies mellow out. I sip my latte, and we chat and laugh. He's gorgeous, but he's a lot more than that. He's easy-going and fun to talk to. He talks about how he grew up reading sci-fi, and although they're not books I've read, with the way he talks about them, I feel his passion for the stories. It makes me want to read some of those books, just so we can discuss them the next time we get together.

Next time? Slow down there, girlie. You have no idea if there's going to be a *next time*.

But I get ahead of myself. I bring out my phone and pull up Amazon. "So, that book you bought. What was the title again?"

"*Destroyer*," he says, the lilt of his voice almost making it a question. "Why?"

"I was just thinking maybe I'd read it, and then we could, I don't know, get together and talk about it or something." I squeeze my eyes shut again. Why does my mouth do that to me? My brain had not caught up yet to tell my mouth to zip it.

When I peek at him, he's smiling and holding out his book.

"Oh, no, I couldn't," I say. "You already bought me these, and coffee."

"Take it," he says. "I'll grab another copy. Like you said, we can both read it and get together again to talk about it."

My tummy does half a dozen backflips (I bet you didn't know tummies could do that). I'm so grateful I drank all my coffee, because there's nothing to spill when I bang the book against the mug in my attempt to take it out of Alex's hand.

"Thank you," I say. "This is really nice."

Alex smiles again and my brain melts, like butter in a hot pan.

"Well, if we're going to do a buddy read of *Destroyer*, I suppose I need to be able to contact you when we're finished." He pulls out his phone and raises his eyebrows.

It takes me approximately five seconds longer than a normal person to answer, and his face is starting to look worried by the time I sputter out my number.

He meets my eyes, holding my gaze for a long moment, and smiles that brain-melting smile again. "Do you like texts or phone calls?"

"Texts. I never answer my phone. But I will if it's you calling." Oh god, I did it again. What is *wrong* with me?

But Alex just chuckles softly and types something on his phone. A second later, mine dings with a text.

"There," he says. "That's me. We'll read this and make plans to get together again when we're done."

I lift my phone and stare at the number. What kind of alternate universe am I living in? "Okay, sounds perfect."

"It does, doesn't it?" he asks.

I lift my eyes again to the ceiling in a silent plea that I am not, in fact, dreaming. And if I am, that I never, ever wake up.

9

MIA

Shelby's house is about a thirty-minute drive from the bookstore. I keep glancing at the bag with my pile of new books, wondering if that actually happened. I'd almost be able to talk myself into believing that it didn't, but I can see *Destroyer* peeking out from the opening.

Yes, that did actually happen.

I take a deep breath when I turn off my car in Shelby's driveway. I check my phone and look at Alex's text again. It's just a little winky face emoji, but all I can see when I look at it is the wink he gave me when we said goodbye.

Alanna comes barreling down the hallway as soon as I walk in the front door.

"Hey, pretty princess." I crouch down so I can gather her up in a big hug.

"Hi Auntie Mia," she says. Her pronunciation is getting better—she used to call me Auntie Mi.

Shelby waddles down the hallway toward us. I'm not being mean when I say she waddles, although it *is* kind of fun to see her like this. When she's not almost nine months pregnant, she's so damn graceful, she might as well be a cat.

"Hey, sissy." She hugs me as best she can with her belly in the way. "Thanks for coming over."

"Of course."

Alanna takes my hand and drags me toward the kitchen. "Can we bake cookies? Please?"

"She's been asking me to bake cookies all week, but I'm too tired," Shelby says.

"We can definitely make cookies," I say.

Shelby sits in a dining chair that she has pulled up near the entrance to the kitchen. The sink is full of bubbles, and plastic bowls and cups are strewn around the wet counters.

"She wanted to play doing dishes," Shelby says. "I didn't have the energy to refuse."

I laugh and start wiping down the counter with a towel. I step toward the stove and my foot slips in a puddle of water on the floor. I grab the counter to keep from falling and knock over a plastic mixing bowl. It bounces across the floor, and Alanna giggles.

"What's up with you?" Shelby asks. By her tone, I know it's not a small talk kind of question.

I tuck my hair behind my ear and smooth down my shirt. "Nothing. There's water on your floor. I slipped."

"You seem really edgy," she says. "More than usual, I mean."

"I'm not usually edgy," I say.

"Yes, you are," she says. "But what's going on? Is everything okay?"

I take a deep breath. "I'm not edgy. I just... I kind of had a crazy morning."

"What's going on?" Shelby asks.

I shoot her a scowl.

"Come on," she says. "Daniel is working six days a week right now, I'm so pregnant I get winded walking up the stairs, and I'm cooped up at home with only a four-year-old to talk to. I just want to have a conversation about something other than princesses and poop."

"Okay. I went to a book signing this morning and I kind of met someone at the bookstore."

"Someone?" she asks. "Do you mean, someone like a man?"

"Yes, obviously that's what I mean."

Shelby sucks in a breath so hard she almost squeals with the effort. "Oh my god, tell me *everything*. Alanna, honey, you can have thirty minutes on the iPad if you want so Mommy can talk to Auntie Mia, okay?"

Alanna runs off to the living room to play on the coveted iPad, and Shelby levels her gaze at me.

"Spill it, Mi."

"You aren't going to believe this. I bumped into him—don't roll your eyes, it was really crowded. Anyway, he helped me pick up my books and then he offered to buy them for me."

Shelby looks confused. "Why would he do that?"

"I don't know, it was kind of like offering to buy a girl a drink, but he bought my books. Seriously, it was amazing."

"I guess he already knows the way to your heart."

"Exactly," I say. "Afterward, we went out for coffee."

"And..."

"And it was fun, and I gave him my number, and he said he wants to get together again," I say. "He gave me his copy of the book he was buying so I can read it. Then we're going to get together and talk about it once we've both finished."

"Huh," she says.

"Why do you look so skeptical?"

She shrugs. "I don't know. That just sounds so... not sexy."

"Shelby, you have no idea. He's beyond sexy. He's so gorgeous, I have no idea why he was interested in me."

"Whatever, you're pretty in your own way," she says.

I roll my eyes. I know Shelby, and she meant that as a compliment. But it still sends a flash of annoyance through me. "Well, I'm telling you, he was a freaking dream."

"Do you have a picture? I want to see."

"I don't, but maybe I can find him on Facebook or something."

I search his name and find him immediately. Alex Lawson. His profile picture is him in a pair of sunglasses, his lips parted in a smile. Seeing his face makes my heart beat faster. I scroll down and find more photos he's posted. I get to one of him standing on a beach holding a beer and I start coughing. He has his shirt off, and *oh my god*.

"What?" Shelby asks, holding her hand out. "Show me. I don't want to stand up and I certainly can't chase you."

I hand her my phone and she flicks across the screen with her thumb, her eyebrows raised. "Wow. Okay, you're right, he's gorgeous. But this guy? Bookstore?"

"Yes, this guy, in a bookstore," I say.

She holds my phone out to me and I take it, putting it in my back pocket. There's a good chance I'm going to stare at those pictures again later.

"That's awesome, Mia," she says. "When are you seeing him again?"

"I'm not sure," I say. "Soon. I guess we need time to read the book. He's going to text me."

"Well, if he doesn't come through, let me know," she says. "My neighbor down the street has a brother and—"

"Nope." I put my hand up. "Not letting you set me up."

"Why not?"

"Because I hate blind dates with all the fury of a thousand suns."

"Drama queen," she says. "But really, I'm excited for you. At least he's real and not some book boyfriend or whatever. I swear, reading so much has ruined you for real men."

"It has not," I say.

She raises her eyebrows. "You broke up with what's-his-name because he teased you about reading so much."

"That isn't the only reason I broke up with him," I say. "Besides, it was irritating. I don't have to put up with that."

"Men are generally irritating," she says. "You should get used to it."

"You're just grumpy because you're ready to pop that baby out."

"Probably," she says. "But keep me posted. I want to hear all about your next date."

"I know. I'll tell you," I say. "For now, how about you go upstairs and take a nap. I'll clean up and help Alanna make cookies."

"You are a saint, do you know that?" she asks. "There are no better words a pregnant woman can hear than *why don't you go take a nap.*"

Shelby goes upstairs and I get the worst of the water mess cleaned up. I bring Alanna in the kitchen and we spend the next hour messing everything up again. We get the cookies in the oven, and I send her off to play in the living room while I do the dishes. The last thing Shelby needs is to come downstairs to a worse mess than when she left.

By the time Shelby gets up, the cookies are done and their sweet scent fills the house. I sit with Alanna and play tea party, nibbling on a cookie with my pretend cup of tea. But I'm getting increasingly anxious to go home. I want to make sure I read this book before Alex texts me again.

I stay until Daniel gets home, shortly before dinner. They invite me to stay, but I make an excuse about needing to feed

Fabio. I head back to my apartment, and no sooner do I have my cat fed than I'm on the couch with my new book.

I settle in to read, and it isn't long before I'm caught up in the story.

Although not so caught up that I don't take intermittent breaks to stare at Alex's picture again.

10

ALEX

*M*y phone dings with a text just after I step out of the shower. I run the towel over my hair and wrap it around my waist. I have a feeling it's Kendra. I'm hoping it isn't Mia. At least, I'm hoping it isn't Mia saying she has to cancel our date tonight.

I texted her a few days after we met at the bookstore, asking how much time she needed to finish the book we were both reading. I figured she'd need another week or so, and had decided to just ask her out to dinner in the meantime. I didn't want to wait that long before seeing her again. But she texted me back to tell me she'd read the entire thing already. I had only read about half, but I resolved to finish it that night, and made plans to get together with her for coffee the next day.

I met her at a little café over on Queen Anne and we spent several hours nestled at a corner table by the front window, just talking. We talked about the book, but once we'd chatted about the plot and the characters—things we liked, things we didn't, how it ended, that sort of thing—we just kept talking. The only reason we left was because the café closed at four. I was kicking myself for not suggesting a place that was open into the evening. I didn't want to leave.

At first, Mia seemed uncomfortable, even stiff. She knocked her book off the table twice in the first ten minutes, and I could tell that she was flustered. But I caught the book before it hit the floor the second time, and used handing it to her as an excuse to touch her hand. After a while, we got lost in the conversation, and her body language completely changed. She stopped fidgeting and adjusting her glasses. Her hands moved when she talked, but she didn't seem so preoccupied with them.

We chatted and laughed and when the staff started stacking chairs on the tables, we reluctantly got up and left. I really wanted to kiss her outside the café, but she kept wringing her hands together, acting nervous again. I didn't want to come on too strong. Instead, I asked if I could take her to dinner on Saturday, and she quickly agreed.

Tonight, I'll definitely be kissing her. It's a question of *when*, not *if*. As for more, that's up to her. I'm not one to push a woman into something she's not comfortable with, and we haven't known each other long.

But there's something about her. When we had coffee, I couldn't stop staring—at her smooth skin, her bright blue eyes, her soft lips. Maybe writing books with a lot of sex in them has changed how I think—or maybe I'm just a guy—but I couldn't stop fantasizing about her. I wonder what her skin tastes like. What she looks like when she comes. She's not quite the *girl with glasses hiding a sex kitten underneath*—there's plenty of that sex kitten showing, glasses or no. But I still feel like she's keeping a bit of *bad girl* inside—maybe waiting for the right guy to bring it out.

I'd love to be that guy.

I check my phone and, sure enough, I have a text from my sister.

Kendra: Plans tonight?

Me: Yes, I have a date.

I chuckle to myself, knowing that's not the answer she's expecting. I haven't told her about Mia yet. Mostly, I'm waiting to see if this seems to be going somewhere before I let Kendra get too excited. But I might as well tell her what I'm doing.

Kendra: You do not. Who? Since when?

Me: Yes, I do. Her name is Mia. Since the other day when we had coffee and I asked her to dinner.

Kendra: Why didn't you tell me, you shit? When can I meet her?

Me: We just met, so calm your ass down.

I finish getting ready, opting for a light blue button down and dark jeans. I grab a jacket and head out to pick up Mia. We drove separately and met at the café the other day, but tonight I'm picking her up.

When I get to her building, I park out front and buzz her on the intercom. She comes out a minute or so later, dressed in a dark red shirt, black pants, and tall boots. She's still trying to put her coat on as she walks out the door, but she can't seem to get her arm in the sleeve.

I step behind her and hold out her coat so she can slide her arm in. She glances at me with a shy smile and I help pull her hair out from the back of her coat. It's silky soft, and standing this close to her, I get a hit of her scent. I don't know what kind of pheromones this girl is putting off, but she's intoxicating.

"Thanks," she says.

I drive us toward downtown and luck out, finding a parking spot near the restaurant. We head inside List, a trendy Italian place in Belltown. The ambiance is great for a date; it's cozy and intimate with dim light emanating from red chandeliers.

The host takes us to our table and I help Mia with her coat. We sit and the waiter takes our drink orders—pinot noir for Mia and a glass of Maker's Mark for me.

Mia peruses the menu, but I see her looking at me over the top of it, like she's sneaking glances.

"What are you thinking?" I ask.

"That I can't believe this dream hasn't ended yet."

I laugh. "What dream?"

She hides behind the menu for a second. "I meant... No... I didn't mean..." She takes a deep breath. "This dream where I'm here with you. It kind of feels like I've been dreaming since that day I crashed into you in the bookstore."

"I don't think it's a dream. But if it is, at least it's a good one."

"Yeah, definitely a good one. I'm sorry, I think you meant what am I thinking of ordering, didn't you?"

I smile. "I did, but I like your answer better."

"I don't know, it all looks good," she says.

"We could just order a bunch of stuff and share it all," I say with a shrug.

She lets her menu drop to the table. "That sounds perfect."

"Really?"

"Yeah. Why, were you not serious?"

"No, I was. Sorry, you caught me by surprise. I love doing dinner that way. But, let's just say it's been a while since I was out with someone who shared my enthusiasm."

"I guess you weren't out with the right person." As soon as she speaks, she clamps her mouth shut, like she didn't mean to say that. She does that sometimes, and it's adorable, like her mouth gets ahead of her.

"Obviously I wasn't out with the right person," I say. I almost finish with, *because I wasn't with you*, but our waiter arrives with our drinks.

The waiter takes our order. Mia insists I order whatever I want and we'll both share everything. It's such a small thing, but my ex hated to share her food, so we never did this together.

Mia takes a sip of her wine. "Okay, I think we're at the point where you need to tell me about her. And then I'll tell you about mine."

"About who?"

"About your ex," she says, her tone matter-of-fact. "I can tell you have one. I mean, who doesn't, right? But I can tell you have one that still matters somehow."

"How can you tell?"

She shrugs. "You've been surprised a few times by things I've said. Not surprised like, *what's wrong with her?* Although I get that a lot. It's more like, *wow, the last woman I was with sure wouldn't have done that.*"

"I'm completely transparent, aren't I?"

"I'm sorry," she says. "I shouldn't have said all that. Sometimes I get ahead of myself and say things, and... I don't know. I'm not good at this."

"No, you're fine," I say. "You're absolutely right, there's an ex, although I wouldn't say she still matters. But, to be totally honest, I was married to her."

"Ouch. How long has it been since, you know?" She mimics pulling a ring off her finger and tossing it over her shoulder.

I laugh and take a sip of my drink. "We've been divorced for a couple of years. She moved out quite a while before that, though. And Mia, she's not in the picture. At all. I haven't spoken to her since the divorce was final."

"I wasn't worried about that," she says. "I dated a guy once who wasn't over his ex, and believe me, you don't have that air about you at all."

"Well, that's good. So what about yours?"

"My what?"

I laugh again. "Your ex. Wasn't this an *I'll tell you mine if you tell me yours* deal?"

"Oh, right," she says. "I didn't marry him, thank God. It's been about a year since we broke up. He was... irritating."

"Irritating?" I ask. "How so?"

"He teased me a lot," she says. "Not cute teasing. He meant it. He'd make fun of me whenever I did something clumsy, and he gave me a bad time about how much I read. My sister Shelby said I was too hard on him, but honestly, who has time for that?"

"You're absolutely right," I say. "You shouldn't ever let a guy treat you that way."

"That's what I said. I guess Shelby teases me for the same things, so maybe that's why she didn't think it was such a big deal."

"Tough relationship with your sister?" I ask.

"Yes, and no," she says. "I love her, and she means well. She's just... overly critical. She's as critical of herself as she is of me, though, so that's kind of how she is. A quintessential oldest child."

"I'm the oldest child, and I don't think I'm overly critical of my sister."

"Maybe not, but have you asked your sister?" She closes her eyes for a second. "Sorry again. That just kind of came out. You don't actually seem like the overly critical type."

I smile. Her honesty is so refreshing. I feel like I'm looking right at her, and seeing nothing but the real Mia. There's no mask. No games. "Actually, you make a good point. Kendra might think otherwise. But she and I have a pretty good relationship."

"Do you have any other siblings?" she asks.

"Yeah, I have a younger brother, Caleb. He lives in Houston so I don't seem him very often. He's a single dad, so he's really busy."

"Wow, I'd imagine so."

The waiter arrives with our food. He sets the first two plates down and we both move our drinks to the side to make room. Mia reaches across to get her silverware out of the way and bumps her water glass. It tips over with a clink, spilling water onto the table.

"Oh no. I'm so sorry." She starts to scoot back, but there's someone seated right behind her.

I reach out and place my hand over hers before she moves, gently stopping her so she won't bump into anybody. The waiter already has most of the water cleaned up; he was quick with his towel. I keep my hand on hers, and carefully tip her glass upright. "It's all right. We're good."

She swallows, her eyes locked with mine. The waiter clears his throat and I let go, moving so he can set the rest of our dinner on the table.

"Thank you," she says.

I'm not sure if she means me, or the waiter, but her eyes are on me.

We dig into our food, and everything is delicious. We have calamari, gnocchi, bacon wrapped prawns, and spicy meatballs, plus fresh bread. We talk while we eat, and we both laugh a lot. She tells a story from when she was sixteen—she jumped into a pool and lost her bikini top in front of her crush. I find myself telling her about the time I ripped my pants open trying to hop a fence while fleeing a high school party. She laughs so hard her eyes tear up, and then apologizes profusely for laughing. But I can't stop laughing either.

After dinner, we share a bowl of chocolate gelato. Mia rolls her eyes and moans with pleasure every time she takes a bite. It's such a turn on, I stop eating, just so she'll have more and I can watch her enjoy it.

She doesn't protest when I take the bill from the waiter—just smiles and thanks me. Is it really this easy? No squabbling over who should pay, or what it says about our society that I want to. She simply appreciates my gesture for what it is.

I help Mia into her coat again before we leave. This time I

don't wait for her to start pulling her hair from the back of it; I slide my hand across the back of her neck and lift her hair so it hangs outside her coat. I'm not ashamed to admit, I smell her again while I do it. God, this woman smells good.

I put my hand on her back, just below her waist, as we walk out to my car. I'm being a little aggressive, touching her so much, but I want to show her that this door is wide open.

If she's not ready for this date to end, then neither am I.

11

MIA

*T*hat thing about dreaming? Still doing it. Still don't want to wake up.

I think I just had the best date of my entire life. The restaurant was adorable, the food was amazing, and the date himself? He's a walking dream.

Alex leads me toward my apartment door, his hand firm on the small of my back. I'm nothing but a great big zinging nerve. I relaxed during dinner, but now I'm back to jittery, can't-make-my-limbs-work-right Mia. My toe catches on, well, nothing, and I stumble. Alex casually grabs my arm to steady me, but doesn't make a thing out of it. It's like he barely noticed that I almost fell flat on my face.

We stop outside my door and my heart beats faster. I hope this burns calories, like doing cardio, because I am getting *such* a workout right now.

And I need it after all the gelato I just ate.

Alex's hand is still touching my arm and his fingers glide over my elbow when he lets go. I turn so we're facing each other. I should get out my keys, but my hands don't seem to remember what to do. Fabio starts scratching the door from the inside. I guess he can smell me. Great, now I have to explain *that*.

"Sorry, I have a cat. He's kind of an asshole."

Alex laughs. "They usually are."

Oh no, does he not like cats?

Let's not get sidetracked. Keys, Mia.

But the way Alex is looking at me is so distracting, I can't remember where I keep my keys. His eyes drill into me, and suddenly I'm thinking about other things drilling into me too. Wow, that's one hell of a fantasy to have while my date stares at me in front of my door. I swallow hard and lick my lips, then realize the way my chin is lifted and my tongue just gave him a little show, I probably look like I'm getting ready for him to kiss me.

My brain is trying to catch up and stop me, but I tell it to go away.

"I had a great time tonight," he says, his voice soft.

Fabio answers with another round of scratches. I barely resist the urge to kick the door.

"I did too. A really great time."

He smiles and steps in closer, his eyes never leaving mine. I'm afraid to move; I'll probably step on his foot. But he closes the distance and I keep my face angled toward his. He leans down, tilting his head slightly, and places his lips against mine.

His kiss is soft at first. My eyes close and the tension in my body melts away. When his hands come to my waist, I put mine on his arms and there's no clumsiness. I simply touch his forearms, my brain and body working together for once.

We reach the point where he could pull away and this would have been a perfectly nice first-dinner-date kiss. But pull away he does not. He presses his lips together like it's over, then surges in, his hands tightening on my waist. His tongue brushes against my lips and I surrender to the heady rush of kissing him.

He parts my lips and his tongue slides against mine, slow and sensual. He tilts his face, draws my body against him, and kisses me so deep, I totally lose track of where I am. Sparks fly behind my eyes, little pings of light racing through me, tingling every nerve ending. I clutch his arms, digging my fingers into his tense muscle. Every thought flees and there's nothing but his stubble scratching my skin, his mouth tangled with mine, and his arms holding me close.

His movements slow and I start to come back to myself. His grip on me loosens and his lips hesitate, still locked with mine. I don't want him to stop, but after the space of a breath, he separates from me.

It takes a long few seconds for me to even open my eyes. I'm dazed—completely intoxicated. No one has ever kissed me like that before. So perfectly. I didn't even mess it up. Normally I get so flustered, I do things like elbow the guy or poke him in the eye.

But not this time. Not with Alex.

His eyes are a little glassy and I get the feeling he's as dazed as I am. His mouth turns up in a small smile and he still has his hands on my waist.

I should invite him in. My lady parts are giving me all the right signals, sending a constant stream of *get this man between your legs* messages to my brain. My heart is racing, and the surge of heat that hits my core makes it hard to form a coherent thought other than *take me now*.

Just as I open my mouth to offer, Fabio howls through the door. Don't think a cat can howl? You haven't met Fabio.

It breaks the spell and my body feels like I'm all awkward limbs again. I can't decide if I should ignore my asshole of a cat and kiss Alex again—he's just watching me, like he's waiting to see what I do—or step back and say something. In the end, I get all tangled up, doing a combination of both, and all I manage to do is step on Alex's foot.

"Oh god, I'm so sorry." Fabio howls again and this time I *do* kick the door. "Shut it, Fabio."

Alex drops his hands and takes a step back. "It's okay."

Great. That kiss practically scorched my panties off and I already ruined the moment. I start fumbling in my purse for my keys. "I... this was... I should probably go in and deal with my pussy... Oh god... I mean my cat."

He laughs, but steps away—nonchalant, like this is exactly how he saw the date ending. "All right. I should let you get to your... *cat*. I'll text you, okay?"

My heart sinks, straight through my stomach, down my legs, and into my feet. But I do my best not to let it show. "Yeah, that would be great."

He waits while I unlock my door, but makes no move to ask to come in. Which is good, right? He kissed me like he could ravage the rest of my body, but he's not going to push it. That's a gentleman move.

Except I'm afraid it's not. I'm afraid he just decided my weirdness isn't worth it.

"Goodnight, Alex." I open the door and shove my foot in the crack so Fabio doesn't get a bee up his ass and bolt into the hallway to find out what's been taking me so long. He doesn't— just twitches his tail up and walks toward the kitchen, supremely confident that I'm coming in to feed him.

"Goodnight, Mia," Alex says with another smile. Then he turns and walks away.

I head into my apartment and shut the door, then lean against it with a heavy sigh. That's such a cliché, but now I understand why people do it. Especially after being kissed like *that*.

And I had to go and mess it up. Figures.

I wonder if Alex *will* text me. Our first real date and I spill water, say who knows how many awkward things during dinner, and choke in the big moment at the end.

Fabio meows.

"I blame you, little shit. What was with the howling, anyway? You're not starving."

I drop my purse on the counter and fill his cat dish. Stupid asshole cat.

A hot shower sounds nice, so I indulge in a little bathroom pity party. The water relaxes me at least. When I get out, I don't feel like I'm going to trip over everything in sight. I towel off and put on sweatpants and a t-shirt, then make some tea and settle in on the couch with my laptop.

I suppose I'll just have to wait to see if Alex decides to text me. I want to vent about my embarrassing evening, but if I call Shelby, she'll just tell me all the things I did wrong. She means well, but her idea of "listening" is to point out all my flaws and come up with detailed plans of how to make me better. I don't need that big sister stuff right now. I just need to vent.

I bring up messenger to see if Lexi is online. She's always good at making me feel better after a disastrous date.

Granted, this *wasn't* disastrous. Not at all. And that's the really disappointing part. I loved it. I had so much fun with Alex, and for most of the evening, things were so easy with him. I stopped stressing about what my hands and feet were doing, and enjoyed myself.

And of course, there's The Kiss of Sheer Amazingness.

Lexi is online, so I shoot her a message then settle in on the couch and await her reply.

12

ALEX

*A*fter dropping Mia off at her place, I head home. I'm a little disappointed our evening ended, but when Mia got her keys out, I decided not to push it. I'd have loved it if she invited me in, and my dick is rather angry at being left out of things tonight. But she got so nervous at the end. It didn't feel like the time to pursue more.

She's such a puzzle. I've never met a woman like her. My ex was completely preoccupied with her appearance, to the point of obsession. Sure, Janine looked nice all the time—polished and put together. But she was more like a mannequin than a real person.

Mia is so... alive. And she doesn't seem to realize how beautiful she is. I never once caught her sneaking glances of herself in windows, and she didn't go to the restroom to touch up her makeup (she was hardly wearing any). I bet it took her all of ten minutes to get ready for our date. But she looked amazing. She doesn't need to fuss over herself to look gorgeous. She just *is*.

I get to my apartment and head inside. It's not very late, so I settle into my office chair and turn on my laptop. I put my hands behind my head while it boots up. That was the best date I've had in a very long time. I lick my lips. A hint of her taste is still on them. That kiss was incredible. You hear people talk about chemistry—hell, I write about it all the time—but I don't think I've ever felt it before Mia. Not really. I've been attracted to women, but what I felt when I kissed her was something else. It was more. It was electricity racing through me, my entire nervous system lighting up. It was a flood of endorphins, and I'm still swimming in them.

The only disappointing part about that kiss was that it had to end.

I'm in no mental condition to be productive, so I open Lexi's Facebook account. A few minutes later, I get a message from BB.

BB: *Hey, Lex. You around?*

Me: Yep, I'm around. What's up?

BB: *Ugh. I had such a night.*

Me: Uh-oh. What's going on? Another bad blind date?

BB: *No, actually. A date, but not a blind one. And the date itself wasn't bad at all. It was great.*

Me: This sounds promising...

BB: *I thought so too. He's kind of amazing. He's gorgeous and so sweet. Honestly, he's so far out of my league I don't know why he's even interested.*

Me: Oh come on, BB, don't say stuff like that. He's lucky to be with you!

BB: *Thanks. I really, really like him. But I think I screwed up.*

Me: What happened?

BB: *Well, he took me out to dinner. We've seen each other before, but this was our first dinner date.*

I watch the screen while she keeps typing. That's a funny coincidence. We both had a first dinner date tonight.

BB: *We had such a great time. I was kind of awkward, and I spilled water once. But he didn't seem to mind. He drove me home and walked me to my door, and then...*

She pauses again and my heart starts to beat faster. Wait, spilled water? This is getting weird.

Me: And then?

BB: Then he kissed me. And oh my god, Lexi, what a kiss. It was unbelievable. I swear, you couldn't have written a better first kiss, and that's saying something. It was a total panty-melting, turn my brain to mush kiss.

Okay, this is freaking me out a little bit. Because I kissed Mia, and if I *was* actually a woman, *panty-melting, turn my brain to mush kiss* is how I would have described it. In fact, that's how I would have written it if it was in one of Lexi's books.

Me: That sounds incredible. But why do you think you screwed up?

BB: Well, afterward I think he wanted to come in. And I really wanted him to. But I was so flustered. You have to understand, IRL I'm a mess. I get so nervous around people, I say stupid things and I'm the biggest klutz. The first time we met, I literally smashed into him and dropped everything I was holding. He has ninja reflexes and somehow caught my half-full cup of coffee while I spilled books all over the floor.

She keeps typing and I wait, my heart practically pounding a hole in my chest. There is no way.

BB: So, tonight, I don't know, that kiss positively melted my brain. And then my stupid cat was howling, and things got weird, and he left. I'm so bad at this stuff. I'm the most awkward human ever. Online I think I come across as fairly normal, but you wouldn't recognize me in person.

I stare at the screen, the reality of this slowly dawning on me. Is this possible? Could BB actually be Mia? I know Mia's a reader, but she's never mentioned blogging. She's never mentioned Lexi either. But why would she? We pretty much just met, and it isn't like she'd tell me about every person she messages online.

There's no way this is a coincidence. Bumping into a guy and dropping her things? Yep, that guy was me. I don't know about ninja reflexes, but I did catch her half-full cup of coffee. Spilled water? Mia did that. Amazing kiss at her door interrupted by a howling cat? Okay, the rest of it I could have called a coincidence —maybe—but there's no way that happened to both of us separately.

She can't have gone on a date that so closely matched mine —particularly the kiss and the awkward ending. It *was* awkward, but I didn't leave annoyed. I left high on the feel of her mouth, and excited for the next time I get to see her.

Apparently it was as good for her as it was for me. But the fact that it was amazing for her too is completely overshadowed by the fact that I think the woman I just started dating is friends with my alter ego.

My female alter ego.

I've gone too long without answering, so I make up a quick reply.

Me: Sorry, bathroom. I'm sure it wasn't as bad as you think.

BB: Thanks, Lexi. You're always so optimistic. I guess I'll wait and see if he actually texts me again. I'm not holding my breath.

Fuck, what do I do now? If Mia finds out who I am—that I'm Lexi Logan—it could risk my entire career. BB has a huge following, and if she outed me, I might not be able to recover. There are a few male romance authors who do well, but it's a tough road for them to get there. And my readers might see it as a betrayal. It's hard enough to stay visible under the best conditions. It's a competitive market. If I do something to mess it up now, I could be screwed.

If this was just about me, that would be one thing. I can always go get another programming job to pay the bills if the writing thing doesn't work out. But *my* bills aren't what I'm worried about. My dad's last MRI bill is still sitting on my desk. I can pay it, and I can make sure we can afford his next surgery without him having to sell the house. But not if my success as Lexi goes away. As popular as her books are, it's precarious. One wrong move, and it could all come crashing down.

I stare at BB's last message on the screen. Not only do I have to weigh the risk to my writing career, dating Mia would be like insider trading. BB shares all kinds of things with Lexi, including dishing about her dates. If I keep seeing her, she's going to talk to me... about *me*. Letting that go on is a dick move. I can't date a woman who is going to confide in me, not realizing she's talking to the guy she's seeing.

When I left Mia at her door, I didn't question whether I'd see her again. I feel bad that she thinks I'm not interested, or that she messed up our date. She didn't. She was... damn it, she was perfect.

But she's right. I'm not going to text her. Just not for the reasons she thinks.

I can't date Mia. I can't get tangled up in a relationship with someone who could conceivably be a risk to my career. I have too much at stake. Telling Mia who I am isn't an option, and how do you date a woman and not mention the fact that you're also friends online?

I close my laptop, a sick feeling in my gut. This is *not* what I want. I want to see her again. She's nothing like any woman I've ever met before. Things between us clicked into place so effortlessly. If she were anyone else—or if I didn't know she was BB—I'd be texting her right now to make plans for another date. Hell, there's a part of me that wants to go back over there, knock on her door, and kiss her until she can't breathe.

But that's a risk I can't take.

13

ALEX

*P*utting Mia out of my mind would be a lot easier if we weren't online friends.

BB messages me a few times over the next several days. Mostly it's just the usual chitchat. She asks about Lexi's latest book, sends me the link to an article about the publishing industry she thought Lexi would be interested in, and sends a few other *non-Alex* related messages.

But then she hits me in the gut with an "update on her date." She tells Lexi she was right, the guy she went out with isn't interested, and he hasn't texted her as promised.

Obviously, I *know* this. But I can sense her disappointment, and it feels pretty shitty. I do my best to reply with something concise but supportive, and hope she doesn't keep talking to Lexi about it.

Thursday I head downtown to meet my dad at Virginia Mason Hospital. He needs another back surgery, in addition to extensive physical therapy afterward. His doctors have high hopes that his quality of life will drastically improve, which is why we're pursuing it. But it's complicated by the fact that his insurance won't fully cover the surgery, and he's been struggling to get approval for the physical therapy. He has to meet with the clinical coordinator to go over the details, as well as the costs involved.

He tried to talk me out of coming, but I know the costs are going to be shockingly high. I want to be there to assure him that I have it covered, and we can move forward with the surgery. The last thing I need is for him to balk and cancel the whole thing.

I sit with my dad in the waiting room, sipping a latte and reading the news on my phone. Dad sits next to me, characteristically hidden behind a newspaper.

A nurse in blue scrubs comes out and smiles. "Mr. Lawson, I'll show you back."

We follow her to a small conference room with a round table. Dad doesn't move very fast with his walker, but he manages. I make sure his chair is steady as he sits down, then take my own seat next to him.

"She'll be right with you," the nurse says before leaving.

We wait for a few minutes, and my dad starts looking at his watch.

"Don't get antsy," I say. "We haven't been here that long."

"I don't like it when they make us wait like this," Dad says.

A woman's voice comes from the doorway. "Ken Lawson? I'm so sorry to have kept you waiting."

I look up and I literally can't believe my eyes. Or my ears. But as soon as I heard the first syllable, I knew who I would see. It's Mia.

Of *course* it's Mia.

I'd say the universe must be trying to throw us together, but I don't believe in that sort of thing. However, this is some serious cosmic bullshit.

Mia pauses just inside the doorway and her eyes widen. She stares at me for a second, her expression a mix of shock and anger. Then she shifts the folder she's holding, adjusts her glasses, and goes around to the other side of the table to sit.

A few papers slip out and float as if caught by a sudden breeze. I catch them before they fall to the floor and slide them back across the table toward her. She reinserts them into her folder without looking at me.

She introduces herself to my dad—who seems to have no idea of what's transpiring between me and Mia. He explains that I'm his son, but Mia still doesn't look directly at me.

I can't blame her for being mad. I blew her off. And although I know I had my reasons, I'm having an increasingly hard time remembering why they seemed so important.

Mia holds me spellbound. I watch her mouth move, barely registering what she's saying—which isn't good, because this is important for my dad. I try to focus on her words; she's talking about the various stages of the process, from surgery to rehabilitation and physical therapy. But all I can think about is what it felt like to kiss her. I want to pull her out into the hallway, push her up against the wall, and kiss her again.

I hear more words I should be processing—something about the option for home nursing care after the procedure. Dad answers a few questions and I nod along, doing my best to keep up with what's happening. Mia slides a few forms across the table toward him, leaning forward slightly as she does. It puts us just close enough that I get a whiff of her scent.

I'm in big trouble.

It's as if my entire body is attuned to her. She looks beautiful in a white button-down blouse and blue cardigan, with a silver necklace at her throat, her dark hair down around her shoulders. She licks her thumb before taking another sheet of paper from the stack and the sight of her tongue darting past her lips makes my heart beat faster. It's stupid how much I love the way she smells. I imagine that scent lingering on my sheets after a night of fucking her, and swallow hard. I really need to knock it off. Having thoughts like that while sitting next to my father is the definition of awkward.

"This is the part I don't like," Mia says, her attention still focused on my dad, as if I'm not here. "We have to talk about costs. Your insurance doesn't cover all the costs associated with your surgery, or the aftercare and rehab. You're looking at some pretty big out-of-pocket expenses if you decide to go through with this."

Dad shifts in his chair. "Yes, the surgeon told us that would be the case."

Mia's eyes finally flick to me, briefly, before looking back at my dad. "Your share of the expenses is going to be nearly fifty thousand dollars."

Dad starts to say something, but I cut him off.

"It's fine," I say. They both look at me in surprise, but I meet Dad's eyes and shake my head. "No arguing with me. This is why I came. I needed to know for sure what we're looking at. I'll cover it."

"Alex, you can't," Dad says.

"Yes, I actually can," I say. "And I will. If this helps, it will be worth it a hundred times over."

I try to meet Mia's gaze, but she starts gathering up her paperwork.

"Thank you for coming in," Mia says. "The next step is to schedule your pre-op appointment at the front desk. You can do that on your way out. And Mr. Lawson, I know this process can be overwhelming. Please don't hesitate to call me if you need anything."

She stands, but one of the buttons on her cardigan gets caught on the chair. She yanks it free and gathers up her folder, then shoots me a glare, as if that was somehow my fault.

I help Dad to his feet and he starts shuffling out toward the front desk. Mia hesitates behind him, and I can tell she's ready to run out of the room as soon as he gets out of her way.

Let her go, Alex. You had good reasons for not seeing her again, and those reasons haven't changed.

Fuck those reasons.

"Mia, wait."

She hesitates near the door, but doesn't turn around. My dad keeps walking.

I step closer. "Can I talk to you?"

"I guess, but I'm not sure why you want to," she says.

"I know I said I was going to text you, and I haven't." Damn it, how do I explain this without digging myself a deeper hole? "Things have just been kind of crazy, with my dad and everything. I was questioning whether seeing someone was the right thing."

"Then why ask me out in the first place?" She looks over her shoulder at me. "If you weren't interested, why bother?"

"That's the problem, Mia, I'm very interested." I take another step toward her. "I've been thinking about you all week. In fact, I can't seem to *stop* thinking about you."

Her expression softens. "I thought after the way our date ended that you'd decided you didn't like me enough to see me again."

I won't lie, she breaks my heart a little with that. "God no, Mia. I'm just too caught up in my bullshit for my own good. I probably like you too much."

The folder slips from her hands, but I step in and catch it before the paperwork spills. I look down at her, my eyes locked with hers as I hand it back.

"I'm sorry I didn't text you," I say, my voice quiet in the small space between us. "I should have. Can I make it up to you?"

Her mouth opens, but nothing comes out.

"Do you have plans tomorrow?" I ask.

"No." She shakes her head slowly.

"Then let me buy you dinner."

She takes a deep breath, her eyes still on mine. "All right. Dinner. But it better be somewhere nice."

I grin at her and instinctively move closer. "Absolutely."

We both hesitate, as if neither of us can look away. I touch her chin, keeping her face tilted toward mine, and close the distance. I place a soft kiss on her lips and breathe her in while I slide my finger across her jaw.

Reluctantly, I pull away. "I'll pick you up at seven?"

Her eyes drift open and she blinks a few times. "Sure. Seven. Seven is good."

"Perfect. I'll see you tomorrow."

She nods, clutching the folder to her chest. I have to tear myself away from her to go catch up with Dad. I find him out front, still talking to the receptionist. I make sure he's squared away with his appointments and take him home.

When I get back to my apartment, I toss my keys on the counter and flop down on the couch. I'm not sure how I'm going to navigate this, but I have to find a way. Walking away from Mia feels... impossible. As surprised as I was when she walked in that room, it was a relief to see her again. She was the proverbial breath of fresh air.

Now that I've established I'm going out with Mia again, I need to figure out how to make this work.

First off, I won't lie about anything other than my pen name. If Mia were any other woman, I wouldn't tell her I write romance novels, so this is only slightly different. I'll stick with the same story I tell everyone—I'm a consultant and I work from home. But everything else I tell her will be the truth, both as Alex and as Lexi.

When she messages Lexi, I'll try to discourage her from talking about me. I'll keep my answers short and won't pump her for more information, even if it's tempting to do so. I won't take advantage of the situation. If Lexi doesn't seem all that interested in discussing BB's dates, eventually Mia won't bring it up anymore. That way, I can keep Lexi's friendship with BB separate from my relationship with Mia.

And who knows what will happen between me and Mia. It isn't like I'm expecting to walk off into the sunset with her. Maybe it's ironic that a romance author doesn't believe in happily ever after, but I don't. I save that fantasy for my books. It doesn't work that way in real life—or at least, it doesn't work that way for me.

If things go on long enough with Mia that I can't keep my alter ego from her anymore, I'll figure out how to tell her. But I'll cross that bridge when—or if—I come to it.

My phone lights up with a message. I hesitate before opening it—it's from BB. This should be interesting.

BB: I have had the craziest day.

Me: Have you?

BB: Yep. Remember that guy I went out with and then didn't hear from?

Me: Yeah.

BB: I kind of ran into him today.

Me: Wow. That must have been a surprise.

BB: Right? I know, it was. It was shocking, to be honest. He apologized and asked me out again.

Me: Did you say yes?

BB: Are you kidding? I don't think I could have said no. He completely zaps my ability to think straight. It's like my brain shuts off and it's all hormones and blood flow.

Me: LOL. Sounds like you'll have a good time.

BB: I hope so. He kissed me again and OMG. I'm totally wearing the special panties on this date.

Special panties? What does that—oh. *Oh.* That means she's

up for... I take a deep breath and type a quick reply before she keeps going.

Me: That's awesome, BB. Sorry, but I gotta run. I'll chat with you later.

Well, this got complicated fast. Maybe some guys would congratulate themselves on knowing their date is pretty much guaranteed to have a happy ending. Special panties, indeed. But here we go again with the insider trading.

Obviously I want her. I'm so attracted to her, it was hard to concentrate when I saw her earlier. But can I act on something she tells Lexi? I'm walking a fine line here and I don't want to start this on the wrong side of it.

The solution is simple. I won't sleep with her tomorrow night. I'll take her out, we'll have a good time, and I'll say goodnight.

I'm a patient guy, and I have a strong feeling she's going to be worth the wait.

14

MIA

I'm not sure if it's the wine, or simply the giddiness of yet another amazing date, but I can't stop smiling. There's nothing like a guy who can make you laugh, and Alex and I have been laughing all night.

He made good on his promise to take me somewhere nice, somehow scoring a table at Canlis. I'm not sure how he managed that on such short notice, but the meal was amazing. He was just as charming and swoon-worthy as last time. Plus, I didn't spill anything.

In fact, I've been comfortable all night, from the moment he picked me up until now. We're driving back to my place, and instead of feeling anxious and awkward, I'm relaxed. A little euphoric, even.

I was a mess when I ran into him at work yesterday. When I walked into that room, it took me a second to process what I was seeing. I'd noticed the name Lawson on my paperwork, but the idea that the patient could be related to Alex hadn't even crossed my mind.

But there he was, sitting on the other side of the table from me. It was all I could do to stay focused on my job. I was angry at him for blowing me off, and the fact that he looked so damn good only pissed me off more. I didn't want to feel all weak-kneed around a guy who dissed me. But it's basically impossible not to feel that way around Alex, no matter the circumstances.

Maybe I should have played a little harder to get when he asked for another date, but at that point, I was powerless to resist.

And thank God for that.

I run through my mental checklist as he parks in front of my building.

Bottle of wine? Check.

Shaved legs? Check.

Special bra and panties? Check.

Kitty treats to distract Fabio from freaking out over a stranger? I already had some, but still, that's a check.

Clean sheets? After an emergency run to the laundry room this afternoon, yet another check. A girl's gotta be prepared.

There will be no more awkward Mia at the door tonight. I'm nothing but *ready for a night of mind-blowing sex* Mia.

It's possible I'm a little too sure of myself. But Alex smells like man heaven, and I've had an entire evening of smiles, soft touches, and deep gazes. I am ready.

I unlock the downstairs door and everything below the waist is starting to come alive. I don't care what my asshole cat does, I am *not* messing this up again.

But as soon as we enter the building, I know something is wrong. The entry foyer is dark and the glint of someone's flash-light blinks in the stairwell. Plus, it's freezing. My building is always drafty, but I swear it's colder in here than it was outside.

"It looks like the power is out," Alex says. He gets out his cell phone and turns on the light. "Do you want to go check your apartment?"

"Yeah, I should."

We walk up the stairs by the light of our phones, and I hear a few voices in the hall as we head to my door. My neighbor, Jim, is standing in his doorway, pointing a flashlight toward us. He's in his mid-fifties and lives alone, except for at least five huge fish tanks. I'm always a little paranoid they're going to break and flood the entire floor.

"Hey, Jim, what's going on?" I ask.

"Power's out," Jim says. "Whole building. It's been hours. My fish are going to freeze."

You have got to be fucking kidding me. Am I cursed? Maybe I should have been really bold and asked to go to Alex's place tonight. I bet he has power.

I stop in front of my door and turn to Alex. "I'm sorry about this. I'm not sure what's wrong. The building is old, and stuff like this happens all the time."

He rubs his hands together. "It's freezing in here. Is it this cold in your apartment?"

Fabio scratches at the door. "Yeah, probably." I turn to Jim, who is still standing in his doorway. I guess he's waiting to see if someone comes with news? Who knows. He's a weird dude. "Hey Jim, do you know what the ETA is for fixing this?"

"No idea. But they better hurry. My fish require a precise temperature to survive."

"He's very concerned for his fish," Alex says, low so his voice doesn't carry.

"Yeah, Jim is... he's so nice, but he's a little peculiar," I say. "I guess I should check and see if it's any warmer inside. Do you, um... do you want to come in?"

"Yeah," Alex says. "I should make sure I'm not dropping you off to stay in a freezer tonight."

Or you could come in and warm me up. I almost say it, but thankfully close my mouth before it comes out.

It's no warmer in my apartment. I'm betting the power has

been out since I left, and there's hardly any insulation. Fabio's all kitty-fat and orange fur, so I doubt he's even noticed. He eyes Alex with suspicion, but doesn't get too hostile. That's a relief. He sniffs Alex's shoe for a few seconds and I crouch down to pet him.

"Hey, Fabio." I run my hand down his back and he rubs up against my leg. "Has it been a cold evening?"

He meows and saunters into the kitchen to await his dinner.

Alex shoves his hands in his coat pockets. "It's cold in here, too."

I glance around. There's a bit of light filtering in through the window, so it isn't pitch black. But it's uncomfortably cold. I breathe out a long sigh. I can't stay here tonight. My happy zone isn't so happy as I realize this probably means I should tell Alex goodnight and call Shelby to see if I can come stay over.

"I'm sorry," I say. "I thought we could have a glass of wine or something, but obviously that isn't going to work."

"Do you have somewhere else you can stay tonight?" he asks.

I glance at the time on my phone. It's after ten, and Shelby goes to bed early. "Yeah, I can call my sister. I hate to wake her, but I can go to her house. She has an extra room."

Alex looks at me for a long moment, like he's thinking about something. "Okay, good."

It seems like he might say something else, so I hesitate before bringing up Shelby's number. But he just puts his hands back in his pockets and turns away.

I take a deep breath and steel myself to hear my sister whine at me for waking her up.

Right as I'm about to call, Alex speaks up. "Wait, I do too."

"You do too, what?"

"Have an extra room," he says. "It hardly ever gets used. You're welcome to come stay with me. I understand if you're not comfortable with that, but if you don't want to wake your sister..."

Sleepover at Alex's place? *Yes, please.* "That would be great, thank you. If you're sure you don't mind."

"I'm sure," he says.

"Okay, let me just grab a few things."

"What about the cat?" he asks.

Fabio meows and I go into the kitchen to feed him. "Oh, he'll be fine until tomorrow. He has plenty of built-in insulation."

I grab a few things and put them in a small bag—change of clothes, a tank top and shorts to sleep in, some basic toiletries. My lower half is starting to come alive again at the prospect of going to Alex's place. I'm so glad he offered. We can still salvage this night, despite my stupid apartment building betraying me.

After a few more scratches for Fabio, I head out with Alex. He lives near Greenlake, in a much newer building. Thankfully I see lights on in many of the windows when we arrive. He leads me upstairs to his apartment and shuts the door behind me.

"Sorry, I wasn't really expecting to have a guest tonight." He walks in, flips on a light, and starts picking things up.

His apartment is nice. He has a couch and coffee table facing a flat screen TV on the wall, a small dining area, and a home office near the kitchen.

"You can put your stuff in here," he says, gesturing toward what must be the guest room.

"Thanks." I walk past him into the room and set my bag down on the queen-sized bed. Does he really expect me to sleep in here? Is he just being a gentleman, or is he not a bed-sharer? Or maybe I've misread this situation completely. It wouldn't be the first time.

"You should have everything you need to be comfortable," he says. "And the sheets are clean."

"Yeah, this looks great."

He hesitates, rubbing his chin. "If you're not tired, would you like a drink?"

I breathe out a sigh of relief. I was worried for a second he was sending me off to bed—alone. "I would love one."

Alex goes into the kitchen and pours us two glasses of red wine while I take a seat on the couch. It smells faintly like him—a heady mix of cedar and ginger, and don't ask me how I know that—and I have to stop myself from leaning into the cushions and smelling them.

He hands me my glass, hesitating with his hand still on the stem, like he's waiting to make sure I have it before he lets go. Far from being embarrassed, because he's obviously noticed my tendency to spill things, I'm touched by the gesture.

"Thank you."

He settles down onto the couch and angles his body so he's facing me. My nerves act up again and I take a steadying breath to make sure I don't dump wine down my front when I take a sip.

"So, Fabio?" he asks. "Interesting name for a cat."

I laugh. "I used to sneak my grandma's old romance paperbacks, the ones with Fabio on the cover. I thought it would be a funny name."

"It is; I like it," he says. "You said he's an asshole though. He didn't seem so bad."

"Oh, just wait until he crawls on top of you and paws at your face at six in the morning because he wants to be fed. You'll call him an asshole too."

Alex's eyebrows lift and I realize what I said. I basically just implied we'd be having sex at my place and waking up together the next morning.

He recovers before I do, and deftly changes the subject, like I didn't say anything out of the ordinary. We chat for a little while, sipping our wine. My eyes get heavy and I wonder why he's not making a move.

I set my wineglass on the coffee table, using it as an excuse to shift closer to him. With every minute that ticks by, my heart beats a little faster and the tingle in my core grows. I find myself watching his mouth while he talks, wondering what it would feel like on my skin. I already know his kiss can melt me. I'm ready for another one.

His arm is across the back of the couch, his hand near my shoulder. He plays with a strand of my hair while he talks, and I get the impression he doesn't realize he's doing it. His fingers brush my skin and a spark of electricity races through me. Judging by his quick intake of breath, he felt it too.

My tongue slides across my lips while he sets his wine glass on the coffee table. His eyes don't leave my mouth. He leans in close and pauses for a moment, his lips almost brushing mine.

I move the final centimeter and our mouths connect. Alex surges in, running his fingers through my hair to the back of my head. His hand is firm and he parts my lips with his tongue. He tastes like wine and dreams coming true.

He draws me in closer and I grip his shirt, burning with the need to feel more of him. His other hand slides across my waist, finding the hem of my shirt, and his fingers trail along my skin. His beard is soft and scratchy all at once, and it sends sparks of sensation through my skin.

This is what I've been waiting for all night. My body softens against him—no stepped-on toes, no awkward limbs. Just Alex's mouth, his tongue dancing with mine, his hands all over me. Our breath quickening, hearts beating faster. The urgency as hands reach under shirts, feeling hot skin. Desperation to feel more—to remove these stupid clothes that seem hell-bent on keeping us apart.

He squeezes my breast through my bra and my nipples

harden, tingling with the desire to press against his skin. I pull up on his shirt, trying to get it off him, but as quickly as he started kissing me, he stops.

I gasp at the shock of his mouth leaving mine and open my eyes. He takes his hand out from under my shirt and moves away.

"I'm sorry, Mia," he says, a little breathless. "I don't think we should do this tonight."

My brain is trying to catch up, but it's not the area of my body getting the most blood right now. "What?"

He presses his lips together. "I just... I can't. Not right now."

It feels like I just ran smack into a glass door I didn't realize was there. I fix my glasses and stand up, bumping my legs against the coffee table. Both glasses tip over, but luckily they're empty. "Well, that's humiliating. That was... I thought... never mind."

"Mia, wait."

"No, it's fine," I say, struggling to get past without touching him or falling on my face. "Tonight was... power out... guest room."

He calls for me again, but my eyes burn with tears and I don't want him to see me like this. I don't know what just happened, but I'm flooded with embarrassment. I completely had the wrong idea. He wouldn't have shown me to the guest room if he hadn't planned on me sleeping there. I should have taken the hint instead of throwing myself at him. He probably didn't even want to sit and drink wine with me. Here I am, intruding on his home, keeping him up, and then I expect...

I shut the door behind me and sink down on the bed. Maybe I should just go. But it's the middle of the night, my apartment is the temperature of an ice cream truck, and I didn't drive myself. I'd have to get a cab or something, and then drive up to Shelby's.

Either that, or hunker down with all my blankets and hope Fabio deigns to help keep me warm.

I figure the best thing to do is stay. I'll get up early and leave before Alex wakes up. The last thing I need is *that* kind of morning weirdness. The *hey, we saw each other naked last night* weirdness would have been welcome. But this rejection stuff? Fuck that.

After changing into my tank top and shorts, I peek out the door to make sure there's no sign of Alex. He seems to be in his bedroom—which, I might add, he did *not* show me, and that should have also been a clue. If he'd been wanting to sex it up, he probably would have taken me on a "tour" just to make sure I got a good look at his bed.

I dart into the bathroom, and when I'm finished, I check to be sure the coast is clear before heading back into the guest room. I slip under the covers—they are nice sheets, I'll give him that—and pull out my Kindle. I'm way too keyed up to sleep yet, so I'll read for a while until I calm down.

And in the morning, I'm outta here.

15

ALEX

*G*uilt and blue balls are a wicked combination.

I stare at the ceiling in my room, unable to sleep. I feel like shit for upsetting Mia, but I was seconds away from yanking her clothes off and fucking her on my couch. As I lie here in bed, I wonder if I should have done it. There's no doubt she wanted to. So why hesitate? Why make this complicated?

My mistake wasn't telling her no, or even making out with her. I screwed up well before that. I shouldn't have invited her over here when I'd already resolved I wasn't going to sleep with her tonight.

I fully intended to politely decline an offer to come in when I dropped her off after dinner. I had it all worked out in my head: sweet kiss at the door, a few words about taking it slow so I don't seem like I'm rejecting her, and a nice goodnight. Then I'd stay off Lexi's social media accounts for a few days so I don't hear anything else I shouldn't from BB, ask Mia out again, and let things happen as they may.

Or make things happen. I want her so badly at this point, I think I'd be hard pressed to sit through another meal with her.

But when we got to her apartment and the power was out, I couldn't just leave her. It was cold as fuck, and I could see how hesitant she was to call her sister. I decided I could handle it; she could come over, stay in the guest room, and I could stick to my resolve not to sleep with her. But what my brain tells me I *should* do and what the rest of my body *wants* to do are vastly different things. Then there was the wine, the talking, the little touches. I didn't even realize I was playing with her hair until I brushed against her skin.

Once I started kissing her, I knew I was in trouble. At that point, why stop? Why not let ourselves get swept up in the moment?

It's hard to explain. I gave myself such a pep talk before I picked her up, making sure my resolve to wait was lodged deep inside my brain. Maybe it was some sort of penance for knowing things I shouldn't. Maybe it's my way of justifying not telling her that I know she's BB. But it felt incredibly important that I not let things get too physical tonight.

However, I didn't think it was going to hurt Mia the way it did.

I thought she'd understand I'm trying to be a gentleman, even if she didn't know all the reasons why. But she got up and left so fast, I didn't have a chance to explain.

I'm oh-for-two with Mia at this point, and I'm afraid I won't get a third pitch.

It's been a couple hours since I went to bed, but I'm clearly not going to sleep anytime soon. I get up and head for the kitchen, making sure to walk quietly so I don't disturb her. A sliver of light shines beneath the guest room door. Is she still awake?

I shake my head and keep walking. I don't know what to say to her at this point, anyway.

In the kitchen, I pour myself a scotch. Maybe I'll do some writing. I can't wrap my brain around a romance storyline right now—I'm failing at the story in my own life pretty hardcore—but I can work on my sci-fi novel. That might be a nice change of pace. It's been months since I've even opened it.

Scotch in hand, I turn around and stop. Mia is standing in the hallway, her eyes wide, her mouth open.

"Sorry... didn't know... I just," she says, sputtering the words the way she does when she gets flustered. "Bathroom."

She's staring at me, and it takes me a second to realize I'm wearing nothing but a pair of boxer briefs. I stare right back. She's dressed in a pink tank top and tiny shorts that show... everything. The shirt clings to her breasts, her nipples poking out through the thin fabric. A bit of skin shows between the hem and the waistband of her shorts. Her legs are long with that curve into the hips that's so fucking sexy.

Fuck this. It's after midnight, so technically it's tomorrow, right?

I put my drink down and cross the distance to her. She starts to say something, but I touch my fingers to her lips. "I'm sorry, Mia. I was just trying to make sure we didn't move too fast. I didn't mean to upset you."

"I'm confused," she says. "I thought we were... and you wanted... but then you didn't..."

"No, I did. I do."

"Then, why?"

"I keep trying to do the right thing with you, and wind up doing the wrong thing." I slide my hand around her waist and pull her against me, letting her feel my solid erection against her body. "But right now, all I want to do is fuck you until you can't see straight."

"Yes, please," she breathes.

Couldn't ask for a better invitation than that. I back her up toward my bedroom, kissing her, pulling off her shirt, running my hands all over her soft skin. She yanks off her glasses and drops them in the hallway. Somewhere in the back of my mind I know I should remember where they are so I can get them for her later. I push her through the doorway into my bedroom, catching her when she stumbles, and rip her shorts and panties down her legs.

I pick her up and press her against the wall, our mouths crashing together in a frenzy. We hit hard and something falls to the ground, but I ignore it. Her legs wrap around me and I feel her heat against my cock. I grab her ass and kiss her hard, unleashing all the tension I've been holding in.

She puts her hands in my hair, kissing me like she's frantic. I'm desperate to be inside her. I let her legs down to the floor and shove my underwear down, kicking them to the side.

Her hand is instantly on my cock and I groan. I slip my hand between her thighs and she gasps as I slide against her silky wetness. I stroke her, feeling her body respond. She kisses me again and bites my lower lip.

"Oh my god, Mia, I'm going to fuck you so hard."

We back up toward the bed, still touching, grabbing, stroking, kissing. She bumps into my nightstand and the lamp crashes to the floor, but I couldn't possibly care less. I push her down onto the bed and climb on top of her, kissing her neck while she opens her gorgeous legs for me.

I reach over and fumble for the condoms in my drawer, knocking something else off the nightstand in the process. The box falls to the floor, but I get one and rip it open. It only takes me a second to put it on.

"That's just not fair," Mia says, her eyes on my cock.

"What's not fair?"

"You're literally perfect. You're so gorgeous, and you have that too?"

I smile. "You want some of that?"

"Oh my god, yes," she says.

I grab her wrists and pin her hands over her head. She gasps and her eyes light up. My cock teases just outside her opening and I kiss her mouth, letting my tongue slide against hers. She tilts her hips to take me in, but I make her wait, feeling her urgency grow. I kiss down her jaw, to her neck, still holding her down. Right now, she's mine, and I want her to know it.

"What do you want me to do?" she asks, speaking low into my ear. "Do you want me to beg?"

"You can try."

"Please," she says, and nibbles my earlobe. "Please fuck me."

I slide the tip in, but pull out again.

"More," she says.

In a little more, then out. She sucks in a breath and I do it again.

"Oh my god, you're killing me," she says, almost breathless.

I drive into her and she leans her head back, her eyes closed. I pump my hips a few times, then hold, deep inside her, groaning into her neck. She's fucking fabulous—hot and tight, flooding me with pleasure. I kiss her mouth, reveling in the feel of her pussy wrapped around me.

"Is that what you want, baby?" I ask.

"I've wanted this all night," she says. "But holy shit, it was worth the wait."

I couldn't have said it better. I start off slow, but she's not having it. She rocks her hips, urging me to go faster. I mean to take my time and savor her, but she feels so good, I can't hold back.

I hold her down, her arms still pinned over her head, and fuck her hard. The headboard bangs against the wall and Mia moans with every thrust. The pleasure builds almost to the breaking point. Her body beneath me, her skin against mine, the feel of her pussy—I drive into her, hard and deep. It's fucking perfect.

"Holy shit... yes... right there... oh my god, Alex..."

Her pussy clenches and it almost sends me over the edge, so I slow down. I don't want this to end yet. I let go of her arms and kiss down her neck, past her collar bone, to her tits. My tongue slides across her nipple and she shudders. I take it in my mouth and suck gently while she puts her fingers through my hair. Shifting my hips, I keep thrusting in a steady rhythm, licking and sucking her delicious skin.

I roll us over so she's on top, keeping my cock buried deep inside her. She sits up and runs her hands along my chest and abs. Leaning her head back, she slides up and down my cock. I hold tight to her hips, thrusting up into her. She calls out—I fucking love how loud she is—and grinds against me. I run my hands up her ribcage to her breasts, reveling in the feel of their softness in my hands.

The pressure grows as she rides me. Her eyes close, but I watch, enjoying every second. Her hips tilting back and forth. The glistening wetness at the base of my cock. Her hair cascading down her back, her mouth parted open. She grinds hard against me and bites her lower lip, her fingers digging into my chest.

She leans down and I grab the back of her neck, bringing her mouth to mine. I taste the hint of salt on her lips, feel the warm wetness of her tongue.

I want to take control of her again, so I sit up and flip her onto her back. Her eyes roll back into her head as I thrust myself inside her. I brace myself on top with one hand and grab her ass with the other, sinking my cock deep into her pussy.

"Mia, you're fucking phenomenal."

"Oh my god... Alex... can't think..."

The headboard starts slamming against the wall again, but I don't give a fuck. I pound her as hard as I can, holding nothing back. She calls out, digging her fingers into my back, spurring me on. Her pussy heats up, clenching tight, and I know she's close.

"Come for me, baby," I say through ragged breaths.

"Yes... yes... harder... yes... oh..."

Her back arches, her pussy clamps around my cock, and she cries out her ecstasy. The feel of her coming and the sound of her losing her mind is too much. I explode. My body stiffens, my balls unleash, and I burst into her. I'm groaning, growling into her neck, thrusting, coming so hard I'm consumed by it. My cock pulses, the sensation surging through me like a storm breaking.

I slow down, breathing hard. Mia's arms are above her head, her face tilted to the side, her eyes closed.

"Holy fuck, Alex, what did you just do to me?"

I kiss her before I pull out and take care of the condom. I slide back into bed and gather her up in my arms. Silence settles over us like a blanket. My heart still beats hard but my body is filled with contentment.

Mia lays with her head on my chest, her arm draped over me. I run my fingers through her long hair, brushing it back from her face. I'm so relaxed, it's like I'm floating. Her scent fills me with every breath and the feel of her skin against mine is warm and soothing.

She lifts her head up. "You know what sounds amazing right now?"

"Again?" I ask. "I think I need another minute, but if you want more, I'm sure I can make it happen."

Her mouth hangs open for a second. "After that? Fucking hell, Alex, I didn't think men like you existed. But no, that's not what I meant. I meant pizza."

"Pizza?"

"Yeah, like cheap, greasy pepperoni pizza. And a beer. That sounds so good."

I stare at her. Pizza and beer does sound good. It sounds perfect, as a matter of fact, and I can't believe she just suggested it.

"You're kidding, right?"

Her eyebrows knit together and she chews on her lip. "I'm sorry, that was a dumb thing to say, wasn't it? You just blew my ever-loving mind, and I suggest pizza. I told you, I say the wrong thing all the time. I don't know why I do that."

"No," I say with a laugh. I lean forward so I can kiss her. "Greasy pizza and beer sound unbelievable right now. You don't keep saying the wrong thing. Everything that comes out of that delicious mouth of yours is fucking perfect. But it's two in the morning. I don't think anything is open."

"Actually, I know a place that delivers until three. Alberona's over in Freemont."

Why is it so stunning that this woman—who just blew *my* ever-loving mind, for the record—not only suggests post-sex pizza and beer, but knows a place that delivers at this ridiculous hour?

Probably because if I were in an eighties flick, designing a woman with a computer, I'd have made her.

Actually, that's not even close to true. Left to my own devices, I'd have gotten it all wrong.

"That settles it." I sit up. "I need to find my phone."

I get up and survey the damage in the room. Stuff is knocked onto the floor, blankets and pillows are everywhere. We made quite the mess. But I'll deal with it tomorrow.

The pizza is here in less than thirty minutes, and it's awful in all the best ways. I had beer in my fridge, and we camp out on my bed—with plenty of paper towels because this shit is greasy —eat pizza, drink a beer, and laugh at how ridiculous we are.

When we're both groaning because we're too full, we clear the bed, snuggle up together under the sheets, and drift off to sleep.

16

MIA

*M*y eyes are still heavy, but I reluctantly open them. I'm nestled in a comfortable bed surrounded by soft sheets and a big fluffy down comforter.

I freeze for a second. I *know* this isn't my bed. It isn't one of those mornings where you wake up and wonder where the hell you are or how you got there. I remember everything quite clearly—vividly, in fact. But there's still that second of confusion at waking up in a strange place.

Alex isn't in bed, but by the state of the covers, I can tell he straightened them around me when he got up. Faint sounds come from the other room. Is he in the kitchen? If he cooks me breakfast, I might just fall down on my knees and beg him to marry me, because I know for a fact I'll never meet another man who is so perfect.

No, Mia. Don't actually do that.

Granted, we got off to a bit of a rocky start. From dream dates that were straight out of a book, to thinking he blew me off, and then thinking he didn't want to get me naked...

But last night made up for everything. Before Alex, I thought sex was great and everything, but I had *no idea*. It's like the only chocolate I've ever tasted is a Hershey kiss and Alex is fucking Godiva. That body, and my god, that dick. He's thick, and long enough to be mildly intimidating—and completely worth the risk to the lady parts. There was no fumbling around, trying to figure each other out. He *knew*. Somehow, he knew all the right ways to move, all my secret spots that make me shiver and moan. I roll over and relish that unbelievable *I got the shit fucked out of me last night* feeling. I'm warm and achy in all the right places.

As nice as it is to lie in his bed and remember how he ravaged me (and oh god, his pillow smells like him), I should probably get up. I sit up and straighten my tank top. I never did find my panties, but while Alex answered the door for the pizza guy, I put my tank top and shorts back on. I glance around the room. There's shit everywhere. Somehow we even knocked a picture off the wall. I'm glad the glass didn't shatter, although I'm pretty sure I broke his lamp.

I wonder where I left my glasses. I can function without them; my vision isn't completely hosed, but I do see better when I'm wearing them. I didn't bother looking for them before our bed picnic last night. I guess I feel like I'm not as sexy with glasses on, and I didn't want Alex to be reminded of my nerdi-ness right away. I find them neatly folded and placed carefully on his nightstand. I certainly didn't put them there, which means he took the time to find them and leave them there for me.

Is he even real?

I get up and slip into his bathroom before going out to find him. When I come out, he's in the kitchen, pouring coffee. He grins at me and I literally have to steady myself against the wall.

"Morning, beautiful." He holds out a cup of coffee to me.

"Hey... I mean, hi... I mean..." I pause and try to collect myself. "Good morning."

He hands me the mug, pausing for a second while I get my hands around it, then leans in for a delicious kiss.

"Sleep well?" he asks.

"Yeah, I slept great," I say. He gestures toward his dining table and we both take a seat. "How about you?"

"I did too," he says. "Kind of surprising after middle of the night pizza. But yeah, I had a great night."

I don't think I could possibly be filled with more happy hormones than I am right now. I'm trying so hard not to let my smile get too big, because at a certain point everyone looks dumb with a giant grin plastered on their face.

I'm failing.

"So what do you have planned for today?" he asks.

"I shouldn't wait too long before going home to check on Fabio," I say. "And this afternoon I'm going to hang out with my niece. My sister is mega-pregnant and my brother-in-law works too much, so I go up there and help her out when I can."

"That's nice of you," he says and takes a sip of coffee. "I wish I got to see my niece more often, but she lives in Houston. I need to go check on my dad this afternoon."

"How's he doing?" I ask.

"Not too bad," he says. "He's anxious to get his surgery over with."

"I don't blame him," I say.

"Yeah, me neither." He puts down his coffee and takes a breath. "Listen, I'm not going to do the whole *I'll text you* thing. I'm beyond trying to play it cool with you. When can I see you again? And if the answer is anything other than *tonight*, I'm going to argue with you."

I laugh. "I guess if you aren't playing it cool, I won't play hard to get." Who am I kidding? I'm so far past playing hard to get with him it isn't even funny. "Tonight would be great."

We finish our coffee and both get dressed. I'd like to stay and spend more time with Alex, but Fabio might decide to retaliate if I make him wait too long for his breakfast—specifically by peeing on something. And I don't want to keep Alex from his dad.

When we get to my building, Alex insists on walking me up so he can check on my apartment with me. I hope there's power —and heat. Although another sleepover at his place would be more than fine by me. We get inside and all seems to be in order. The light is on in the hallway, and it's just the usual drafty, not bone-chilling cold.

"Okay, Fabio might be kind of an ass right now," I say when we're outside my apartment. I put the key in the door. "He doesn't bite or anything, but if he hisses at you, don't be offended."

"I think I can handle it," he says.

I open the door and Fabio looks up at me and meows.

"Oh, poor kitty," I say. "Are you going to die of starvation?"

Alex shuts the door behind us and laughs. "I don't think that's an issue."

I put down my bag, take off my coat, and head straight for the kitchen. "No, but he seems to think so. Don't you, you chubby little gato?"

I get Fabio's breakfast and do a quick once over of the apartment to make sure he didn't destroy anything in a display of annoyance at his human slave's absence. He knocked a few books off a side table, but otherwise, no harm done.

"It looks like everything is fine here," Alex says. "What time are you going to your sister's?"

"I'm not sure," I say. "I have to text her."

"I suppose I should go and let you get on with your day."

I adjust my glasses. "Yeah, I guess so."

He steps closer and brushes the hair back from my face. His tongue wets his lips and I can't stop staring at his mouth. He places his fingers gently beneath my chin and brings his lips to mine.

How is it that a simple kiss can feel so incredible? Maybe it's his scruff gently scratching my face, or all the nerve endings in my lips being stimulated at once. Maybe it's the way his tongue slides across my mouth, beckoning me to open for him. There's a thud as something I was holding drops to the floor, but I have no idea what was in my hand. I put my arms around his neck as he kisses me deeper, drawing me close.

His hands slide beneath my shirt and find the bare skin of my back. That little hint of skin on skin contact is enough to make me want more. I run my fingers through his hair and press my body against him, feeling the satisfaction of his erection digging into me.

I grab the waistband of his jeans and tug, backing up through the curtain that separates my bedroom. He follows me in, still kissing me, and pulls off my shirt. In a sudden frenzy of quickening breath and eager limbs, we tear off our clothes and fall onto the bed in a tangle.

He took charge last night—which was hot as hell—but I want a chance to blow *his* mind. I get on top of him and slowly crawl down his body, kissing and licking him as I go. I graze my teeth down the line between his chiseled abs. I dig my hands into his thighs while I kiss his lower abdomen, letting my chin brush the tip of his cock.

"Oh fuck, Mia."

I look up and meet his eyes while I run my tongue up his length. His brow furrows and he groans while I wrap my hand around the base and swirl my tongue over the tip. There's nothing like having this kind of power over a man. I tease and test him, feeling how his body responds.

He's so thick and long, but I'm not one to back down from a challenge. I slide him in my mouth and he groans again. God, I love making him do that. I move him in and out, enjoying the feel of his cock against my tongue. I pick up the pace, sucking a little when I get to the top.

"Damn it, Mia," he says between breaths. "That's so fucking good."

His enjoyment turns me on even more. I plunge down on him in a steady rhythm. He runs his fingers through my hair and thrusts his hips.

"Your mouth is heaven," he says, his voice rough, "but I need your pussy. I need it now."

I pause and look up. Our gazes lock, like he's challenging me to disobey him and keep sucking his cock. I draw him in one last time, just because I can, taking my time. His eyes don't leave mine and as soon as I let him go, he's grabbing me, moving me onto my back, holding me down.

He takes my mouth in a hard kiss. My pussy is pulsing with need, but he's not wearing a condom yet.

"Please tell me you have a condom in your wallet," I say, practically breathless.

"Don't fucking move."

God I love it when he's bossy. He leans down to grab a condom out of his jeans and I enjoy the view. Holy shit, his body. He's lean with perfect lines, his muscles flexing as he reaches down. I lick my lips and watch him slide the condom down over his cock, my whole body tingling at the sight.

He wastes no time, pushing my legs open and thrusting himself inside. He lets out a low moan into my ear as he slides all the way in. He feels unbelievable, filling me like no one ever has before. I'm halfway to orgasm, and we've barely even started.

I wrap my legs around his waist and let him take over. He plunges in and out, kissing my neck, down to my collar bone. I reach up to cup my own breasts and he rewards me with a low growl, watching me with narrowed eyes. He takes my nipple in his mouth and I squeeze my tits while he sucks. It drives us both crazy. His thrusting picks up, and he groans and growls while he laps his tongue against my nipples.

Heat and tension and pleasure swirl through me, building until I'm so consumed I can barely think. He gives me friction and pressure just where I need it. His tongue caressing my skin sends sparks through my whole body. We move together, our bodies in sync, our breath fast.

"Ow, fuck," he says out of the blue. "What the hell?"

It takes me a second to realize what's happening. Alex looks over his shoulder and climbs off me. My lungs empty in a rush at the sudden change.

Then I see it. Or rather, him.

"Fabio, you asshole!" I jump up and try to bat him off Alex's leg. Fabio has his paws wrapped around his ankle and his teeth bared, like he's getting ready to sink them into his calf. "No, Fabio! Get down!"

Fabio lets go and scurries off the bed. I grab a squirt bottle from my nightstand and shoot streams of water at him until he disappears into the other room.

"Oh my god," I say, turning to Alex. "I am so sorry. Did he hurt you? Oh no, this is the worst. Fabio, you jackass, I'm taking you to the pound!"

"It's okay," Alex says, his voice soothing. "It's just a couple scratches."

I brush the hair back from my face and check his leg. He has a few claw marks, sharp red lines standing out against his skin.

"Damn it, you're probably going to leave and never call me again."

Alex slides his hand across my cheek, to the back of my head. "Not a chance. You think I'm going to let a minor attack by an asshole cat stop me from making you scream my name?"

My eyes flit down to his cock. Holy shit. He's still hard.

He nudges me onto my back and pins my arms above my head the way he did last night. He takes control, plunging into me—hard. Over and over, his muscles straining, the cords in his neck standing out. He fucks me with fury, and everything else falls away. I'm throbbing and pulsing, the tension building to a peak. I'm loud, uninhibited, not a care in the world for who might hear me.

He slows down for a few thrusts, drawing it out, driving me insane.

"You ready for this, baby?" he asks.

"Yes... now... don't stop that..."

I'm right on the edge of the cliff, my O just out of reach. Alex thrusts his hips and I feel the telltale pulse of his cock as he starts to come. His body goes rigid, his muscles tense. The sensation shoves me off the edge and I freefall, swirling with pleasure.

"Alex... yes... Alex..."

He grinds against me, his cock throbbing inside my pussy. I'm overcome with waves of bliss. He holds deep inside me until my orgasm subsides and I'm left panting beneath him.

"Holy shit," I say, breathless as he rolls off me. I used to think the simultaneous orgasm was a myth, but that's twice in a row for us. "You are so good at that."

He laughs and props himself up on one arm. "You're not too bad yourself."

"Not too bad?" I ask with a smile. "I'm fucking amazing."

"That's actually true," he says. "You are fucking amazing. Or amazing at fucking. I don't know, but I could do this all day."

I run my fingers down his chest. "Mm, I wish we could. But we have a date tonight, right? Unless I already wore you out."

"Not even close, baby. I can't wait for tonight."

His mouth comes to mine and his kiss is soft and luxurious, his stubble brushing against my skin.

"Neither can I."

17

MIA

Shelby looks like she's ready to lose her shit when I arrive. Me? Let's be honest, I feel amazing. I send her straight upstairs and commence playing board games with Alanna. We move on to puzzles, and by the time Shelby comes down an hour or so later, her face is much more serene.

"Hey," she says, pulling her blond hair up into a messy bun. "Thank you again for coming over. I haven't been sleeping well."

"No problem," I say brightly and place another piece of Alanna's pirate puzzle. She has a thing for pirates now, apparently. "There you go, kiddo. I think you can finish this by yourself. I'm going to go make your mommy some tea."

Alanna finishes her puzzle and Shelby sends her upstairs to play in her room for a little while. I make us tea and bring it to the couch. Shelby sits on one end with her legs stretched out, her hand on her belly.

"So how are you feeling?" I ask. "Or is that a stupid question?"

"No, it's not a stupid question," she says. "I feel like I look. Huge and uncomfortable. It's hard to sleep, but I'll be okay. I don't have too much longer."

"Is it freaking you out not to know what you're having?" I ask. "I don't know if I could wait."

She shrugs. "A little. I kind of like not knowing, though. It's like keeping a secret from myself." She narrows her eyes at me. "Speaking of secrets, something is going on. What is it?"

I suck so bad at keeping things from my sister. I don't even have to say a word. She always knows. I push my glasses back up my nose. "What do you mean?"

"You've been smiling since you got here," she says.

"I can't smile?"

"Sure, you can smile. But you're smiling more than normal, and I want to know why."

Thinking about smiling makes me think of Alex, which makes me smile more. My face warms and I can tell by the look on Shelby's face that I'm starting to blush.

"Now you really have to tell me," she says. "Is this about that guy? Did you see him again?"

"Alex, and yes, I definitely saw him again."

Her eyes widen and a smile steals across her face. "You slept with him, didn't you?"

"There was some sleeping involved. And a lot of *not sleeping*."

She adjusts her grip on her tea. "Oh my god, tell me everything."

"We went out to a nice dinner, and it was amazing. He took me home, and the power in my building was out. It was freezing. I was going to call you, but he offered to have me stay at his place."

"Wow, that's bold."

"Yes, and no," I say. "Actually, he put me up in his guest room and kind of stopped anything from happening."

"Except there was a lot of *not sleeping*?"

"Yeah, that happened later," I say. "I went to bed upset, thinking I'd totally screwed up and misread the whole situation.

But he was just trying to be extra gentlemanly. We both got up in the middle of the night because we couldn't sleep, and..."

"And?"

"And we probably woke all the neighbors," I say.

Shelby takes a deep breath. "Man, I miss that kind of sex."

I gesture toward her belly. "It's not like you aren't getting any."

"Yeah, but sex after you've had kids isn't the same," she says. "We always have to be careful so we don't wake up Alanna. I haven't had wake-the-neighbors sex in years. And don't even get me started on trying to work around this belly."

"That's kind of disturbing."

She laughs. "Yeah, well, it's reality. Daniel is a good sport though. This is so exciting, Mi. When are you seeing him again?"

"Tonight, actually. We both had things going on during the day, so we're getting together for a late dinner."

"Good for you," she says. "I can't remember the last time you looked so happy about a date."

"I've never met anyone like him before. He's... amazing."

"Uh-oh," she says.

"What?"

"You have it bad for this guy," she says. "Watch yourself, Mia. You just met him, and you're getting all starry-eyed already. Don't fall too fast. This is real life, not some romance novel."

"I'm not falling. I have my feet firmly on the ground."

She arches an eyebrow at me. "I don't know if you ever have your feet firmly on the ground. Just... be careful, okay? I'm glad you had noisy sex and all that, but I don't want you getting hurt."

"I know." I take a sip of my tea. Shelby always points out the practical side of things, and I know she's just looking out for me. But hearing her say *you have it bad for this guy* makes me twitchy. I *do* have it bad for him, and realizing that makes me a little nervous. She's right, this is real life. Alex isn't some book boyfriend, and I don't have any guarantee of a happily ever after.

We finish our tea, and Shelby insists she'll be fine for the rest of the day; she sends me home to get ready for my date. Even though my logical side knows my sister's concern is justified, I can't help the giddiness that spreads through me when I get home. Every minute that goes by brings me closer to when I get to see him again. My body tingles with anticipation. Even finding a broken picture frame—no doubt knocked to the floor by the one and only Fabio—doesn't diminish my good mood. I sweep up the glass, daydreaming about Alex the whole time.

Yeah, I might be in trouble.

I have time to kill before Alex picks me up, so I hop on my laptop and write up a book review I've been meaning to get to. I post it to my blog, then answer a Facebook message from a new author who's hoping I'll read her book. We chat back and forth a few times, and then I notice Lexi is online. I can't wait to tell her about Alex.

Me: Hey, Lexi. How's the next book coming?

Lexi: I'm a little behind. Busy. How are you?

Me: I'm awesome, actually. Remember special panties guy?

Lexi: Yeah.

Me: Glad I wore the special panties. Although I don't think he noticed them, now that I think about it.

Lexi: Wow, that's great.

Her answer feels a little clipped, although I'm probably reading too much into it. That's the downside of communicating this way. There's no context or body language.

Me: The whole night was spectacular. Awesome date. And the rest of it was... let's just say, it was book-worthy.

Lexi: Book-worthy, huh? That's awesome, BB.

Me: I like him a lot, and we're seeing each other again tonight. But I'm a little worried.

It takes her several minutes to answer, and I start to wonder if she had to get up from her desk—or wherever it is she's sitting. Finally, I see the little dots indicating she's typing.

Lexi: Worried?

Me: I know this sounds weird, but I'm worried I'm going to fall for him too fast. He's kind of sweeping me off my feet. It's not that I don't think he's genuine, or he's out to play me or something. But I was hanging out with my sister today, and she said I have it bad for this guy. She's completely right. I do have it bad for him, and it's a little scary.

Lexi goes quiet again. She's not usually online if she doesn't have time to talk, but I suppose I caught her at a bad time. I feel bad for going on and on if she's busy.

Lexi: Don't worry so much, BB. Have a good time tonight.

Me: Yeah, thanks Lex. I'll let you get back to your book.

I click out of messenger. Something about that felt off. She did say she's been busy, so maybe she just doesn't have time to chat. But it's disappointing. I've lamented to Lexi about my *bad* dates; it's much more fun to have good news to share. I guess I shouldn't assume that she's not interested. If she's behind on her latest book, she probably has a lot on her mind.

I need to get ready for my date, but let's be honest, I'm low maintenance so I don't need much time. Before I get up, I open my email. My heart skips. I have one from Antonio Zane, a male model who just happens to appear on the cover of Lexi's latest book. He's on a lot of book covers, and he's very popular among romance readers. I emailed him on a whim, asking if he'd be willing to let me interview him for my blog. I never in a million years thought I'd hear back. But there's his name, right there in my inbox.

Every word of his email makes my heart beat a little faster. Not only would he love to do the interview, he'd be happy to meet in person. In fact, he asks if my readers would be interested in getting a behind the scenes look at a book cover photo shoot. He'll be shooting with a photographer in Portland soon and if I'm close, maybe I could come.

Holy shit.

Portland is a three-hour drive. I could totally do it.

Although, it would mean meeting someone in person as Bookworm Babe. I've never done that before. It's one thing to be BB online. Quite another to extend that into the realm of *real life*. But to meet Antonio Zane?

Worth it.

I email back and let him know I'd love to. I'll get the inside scoop on a book cover photo shoot, and I can make sure there aren't any pictures taken of me. I'm sure he'll understand my desire to stay anonymous. Besides, no one wants to see *my* face. But my blog readers are going to love seeing more of him.

What a day I've had. And it isn't even over yet. My phone buzzes with a text from Alex and I can't keep the smile from my face.

Alex: Pick you up in 30?

Me: Sounds good. What are we doing? Need to know what to wear.

Alex: I was thinking Brody's Brewhouse, so dress casual. But feel free to wear special panties if you want.

I laugh. Special panties? It's like he's in my head.

Me: Or perhaps no panties at all.

Alex: I'll be there in 5.

18

ALEX

I pull up to my dad's place and realize I haven't been by to check on him for a while. I feel bad about that, although I know Kendra has been here. I've been spending so much time with Mia, I've let it slip.

Kendra invited me over to Dad's tonight. Our brother Caleb got into town yesterday, so we figured we should all get together while he's here. I know it will make my dad happy to have his kids, and his granddaughter, all under one roof. There's a part of me—possibly a bigger part than I want to admit—that hates the fact that I'm not seeing Mia tonight. But it will be good to spend some time with my family.

Kendra looks up from chopping vegetables when I walk through the door. "Hey, Alex."

"Hey." I nod to her and grab the stack of mail. No new bills. That's a welcome change. "How is he?"

She shrugs. "Same as usual."

I go into the living room to find my dad.

"Hey, Dad."

"Alex," he says over his newspaper. I think he must read the entire paper, front to back, at least twelve times a day. He's always reading one when I come over.

"How are you feeling today?" I ask.

He lowers the paper. "Not a bad day today."

"That's good to hear."

I head back into the kitchen to see if Kendra needs help. The door opens and my brother Caleb walks in. He and I look a lot alike. He's my height, with the same brown eyes and hair, and a trim, muscular build. His four-year-old daughter, Charlotte, clutches his hand and buries her face against his leg when I smile at her.

"It's okay, bug," he says to her.

"There he is," I say and step in to give him a hug, careful not to squish Charlotte. He hugs me back, giving me a pat on the back. "It's good to see you."

"Yeah, you too," Caleb says. Kendra wipes her hands on a towel and gives him a hug.

"What's it been, a year?" I ask. "Charlotte is so much bigger."

Caleb nudges her to walk farther into the kitchen, but she still won't look at us. "Yeah, she's grown. Sorry, she acts shy around people at first. She'll warm up to you."

"Well, yeah, she barely knows us," Kendra says. Caleb raises his eyebrows. "I'm not trying to make you feel guilty. It's just the truth. You live in freaking Houston."

"Actually..." Caleb looks down at Charlotte and brushes her hair back from her face. "We have some news. We aren't in town only for a visit. I came for a job interview."

"Caleb, that's great," Kendra says.

"Yeah, things are looking good," he says. "It's been tough getting through my residency with Charlotte. I think it's time we move closer to family."

"You absolutely should," Kendra says. "You shouldn't be doing this on your own."

Caleb grabs some crackers out of a cupboard and gets Charlotte set up with a snack at the kitchen table. Her brown hair is tied back in a ponytail and she's wearing a pink and purple striped dress.

"Cute dress," Kendra says.

Charlotte gives Kendra a little smile, but doesn't respond.

Caleb touches her gently on the head. "Bug, can you say thank you?"

"Thank you," Charlotte whispers.

"We're working on it," Caleb says.

"She's fine," Kendra says. "Have you guys gone to see Mom yet?"

Caleb scowls, and I don't blame him. None of us enjoy seeing our mother. Our parents split up when we were kids. Unlike a lot of the divorced families we knew, we stayed with Dad, rather than living with our mom. We saw her less and less as the years went by. She's a VP-of-something-or-other at a big company, and was always more interested in her career than her kids. Now that we're all adults, the three of us tend to avoid her.

"I haven't," Caleb says. "I'm supposed to have lunch with her tomorrow."

"Surprised she fit you in," Kendra says. "And on a weekday, no less."

"Yeah, well, I have to go downtown to see her, and she already warned me she only has an hour," Caleb says. "Although it could be worse. She could have invited me and Charlotte to come stay at her place while we're in town, and then laid on the guilt when I said we're staying here. Oh wait, she did that."

"Of course she did," Kendra says with a roll of her eyes.

The three of us get dinner finished and on the table. Dad's in good spirits, which is nice to see. We have a pleasant meal, talking as we eat Kendra's lasagna and salad. Charlotte seems to get more comfortable, and even charms her grandad with a big smile when he talks to her.

After dinner, my dad retreats to the living room with a glass of whiskey, as is his nightly routine. Kendra and I clean up, then hang out with Dad while Caleb gets Charlotte off to bed. When Caleb comes out, Dad declares that he's tired, so the three of us take seats at the kitchen table. Caleb brings us each a beer.

"So, what else is going on with you two?" Caleb asks.

"Alex has a girlfriend," Kendra says.

I shoot Kendra a glare.

Caleb laughs, then raises an eyebrow at me. "She's kidding, right?"

Kendra cuts in before I can answer. "Not kidding. But he won't tell me anything and I'm very irritated about it."

"Why would you assume she's kidding?" I ask.

"I don't know, I just didn't think you were interested in getting involved with someone again," Caleb says. "But if you're actually using the word *girlfriend*..."

"Yeah, I'm definitely using the word."

Mia and I haven't discussed it, but what else would she be? We're dating. Sleeping together. We've been seeing each other every chance we get; I'm going a little crazy at not seeing her tonight. And no matter what other complications are lurking, I'm really into her. How exactly does that make her anything *but* my girlfriend?

Besides, I really like the way that sounds. Like she's *mine*.

"That's great, man," Caleb says and takes a drink of his beer. "Why didn't she come tonight?"

"No, it's not... I didn't... I mean." God, I sound like Mia all of a sudden. But meeting my family is a big deal, and as much as I like the way it sounds to call Mia my girlfriend, I don't know if we're ready for that. "We just started seeing each other. It's a little soon to throw her to the wolves."

"Wolves? I'm hardly a wolf," Kendra says.

I raise my eyebrows at her.

"You're definitely a wolf," Caleb says, winking at Kendra. "Okay, so tell us about her."

"Yes, do tell," Kendra says.

I glare at Kendra again. She's so nosy. "Her name is Mia. She's..." I trail off because I'm not sure what to say. She's beautiful? Hilarious? A fucking sex goddess? "She's great."

"Great?" Kendra asks. "That's all you're going to give us?"

"Yeah, that's kind of a bullshit answer," Caleb says.

"All right, she happens to be Dad's clinical coordinator at the hospital," I say. "But that's not how we met. I bumped into her in a bookstore, and asked her out. She's easy-going and fun. Loves to read and has an asshole cat. What else do you want to know?"

"Is she hot?" Caleb asks, raising an eyebrow.

"God, Caleb, you're such a guy," Kendra says.

"What?" Caleb takes another sip of his beer. "I'm just wondering what she looks like. What's wrong with that?"

"She's..." I trail off yet again. Natural. Mesmerizing. Adorable. Sexy beyond words. "She's really beautiful. Long, thick hair. Gorgeous blue eyes. And the rest of her is... yeah."

Caleb nods with a crooked grin. He knows what I mean.

"She's hilarious," I continue. "You guys would love her. She says the funniest things. Stuff pops into her head and she talks, and then gets all cute and embarrassed, like she didn't mean to say it out loud. It's really adorable."

"Huh," Kendra says.

"What?"

"You really *do* like her," she says.

"You expect me to have a girlfriend I don't like?" I ask.

"No, that's not what I mean," she says. "I just don't think I've ever seen you talk about a woman like this before. You're *really* into her."

Kendra is right—I *am* really into her—although I'd like to direct Kendra's scrutiny elsewhere. It's like she can see something I'm not ready for other people to see. I just smile at her, making it obvious I'm done talking about this. I want to change the subject, but I'm hesitant to ask Caleb if he's seeing someone. His wife died shortly after Charlotte was born, so it's a sensitive subject. Kendra, however, is fair game. "What about you, Kendra? Seeing anyone?"

"Men are the worst," she says. "No."

Caleb smirks. "Maybe you should try a woman."

Kendra laughs. "You have no idea how tempting that is sometimes. I met a guy online recently and we went out a few times. But it was all false advertising."

"False advertising?" Caleb asks. "What does that mean?"

"His profile on the dating site was bullshit," Kendra says. "It took me a few dates to figure it all out, but instead of being a regular guy with a stable job, he's basically a man-child living in his mom's basement, playing video games all day. He claims he's trying to find his passion."

Caleb laughs. "What kind of an ass would think he could lie like that and get away with it?"

I shift in my chair and cough, suddenly uncomfortable.

"Are you thinking about dating at all?" Kendra asks, her voice gentle.

"It's okay, we don't have to tiptoe around it," he says. "I don't know. Being a single dad in med school hasn't left me a lot of time for a social life. I've been out with women a few times, but it's hard. I have to be careful about who I bring into Charlotte's life."

"That makes sense," Kendra says. "No pressure."

Our conversation moves to other things. Caleb talks about the logistics of moving halfway across the country. We fill him in on what's been going on with Dad. He's surprised at the expenses, and says he feels bad for not contributing. But Caleb is sitting under a mountain of student loan debt from going through med school. Once he's finished with his residency, he's confident he'll be earning enough to pay it off and help with Dad. I assure him I have a handle on it. Thankfully Kendra doesn't say anything to make him suspect my consulting gig is anything other than what I've said it is. He's polite enough not to ask how I have that kind of money.

A small voice comes from the hallway. "Daddy?"

"Hey, bug," Caleb says. "You should be in bed." He gets up to get his daughter settled.

Kendra leans in and lowers her voice. "You said Mia loves to read. She doesn't happen to read books by a certain romance author we've both heard of?"

Shit. I don't want to explain this to Kendra. "Uh, yeah, she might."

"Might?" Kendra asks. "Do you know for sure?"

"Fine, yes," I say. "She reads Lexi's books."

"Holy shit," Kendra says. "That's... kind of weird."

"Yeah, you're telling me."

"But you haven't told her it's you?" she asks.

"No," I say. "Of course not. That isn't something you just blurt out on a first date."

"Okay, but you're past the first date," she says. "Are you *going* to tell her?"

"I don't know," I say. "It's not like we've been dating for months and she still doesn't know what I do for a living."

Kendra looks skeptical. "Careful there, Alex. I get why you don't want to just come out and tell the woman you're dating that you write romance novels, but you're walking a fine line."

"It's not that bad," I say. Yes, I realize I'm conveniently leaving out the part about Mia's alter ego being friends with my alter ego. But how do I explain *that* to my sister? "If we keep dating for a while, I'll tell her. I don't think it's a big deal."

"Hm," Kendra says. "I guess. Look, just... don't be a guy about this, okay? I'd hate to see you screw this up."

"You haven't even met her yet. How do you know you aren't going to hate her and *hope* I screw it up?"

"That's actually a fair question," Kendra says. "After Janine, I have very little confidence in your ability to choose a woman."

"Thanks, asshole."

Kendra grins. "But I get the feeling she's nothing like Janine. You've never looked all starry eyed over someone before."

There's that feeling again—that Kendra is seeing something in me that I don't want her to see. "Just don't worry about it. This is why I didn't want to tell you I was dating someone. You're going to over-analyze everything."

"I am not," she says. "I'm just looking out for you."

"Well, thanks, I guess."

She pats me on the arm and gets up from the table.

Kendra goes into the kitchen and I pull out my phone. The green message notification is blinking. I swipe the screen; I have a message from BB. I almost don't open it. If I don't read her messages, I can't get into trouble, right?

But I can't just ignore her.

BB: I'm sorry to bug you, I know you're so busy. But the coolest thing happened recently and I haven't had a chance to tell you about it.

Me: You're not bugging me. What's up?

BB: I scored an interview with Antonio Zane for the blog! Can you believe it?

Me: The model? Wow.

BB: I know. I'm so excited. I was going to send him some questions and he could just write his answers and send them back. But he invited me to come see one of his photo shoots! It's about a three-hour drive, but WORTH IT. I can't even right now.

My brow furrows as I read her message. I'm familiar with Antonio Zane; his reputation precedes him, and he's on a couple of Lexi's book covers. He's basically what you'd expect from a model. Physically perfect, in love with himself, used to women dropping their panties for him. He burns through girls like wildfire in a dry field.

I do *not* like the idea of Mia spending time with him.

But what am I really worried about here? That he's going to bang her at the end of the interview? When I think about it that way, it seems pretty stupid that I'm grinding my teeth together, seething with jealousy. Mia's not like that, even if he is.

But still. She's going to spend a day swooning over Mr. Hot Abs, and the thought of it makes me ragey to a degree that is probably not healthy.

God, I have to reply to BB. What the fuck do I say?

Me: Definitely exciting. Although, you know, I've worked with him. He's known for being difficult. A real diva. It might be easier to get good answers if you just send him your questions.

BB: Yeah, maybe. But do you really expect me to turn down the chance to ogle Antonio Zane in the flesh? HOT DAMN

For fuck's sake, Mia. Would you say that to me in person? Obviously not; you think you're talking to a girlfriend.

It's driving me nuts how weird things get every time I talk to her online. Our conversations never felt the least bit awkward or uncomfortable before. Now every time I see her name pop up, I cringe, wondering what new thing she's going to say to Lexi that I probably shouldn't know. I thought it was bad when she called me *special panties guy*. Now she wants me to gush with her about a model? A guy she's driving three hours to go interview?

And I know what that interview is going to be like. I know

the fans who read her blog. A lot of them are Lexi fans, and I adore those women like you wouldn't believe—but some of them are crazy. Ravenous, horny, man-crazy women who will be shouting virtual encouragement at her to do all sorts of things to, and with, Antonio Zane while she's there. I can only imagine the messages she's going to get. They'll tell her to see if she can be the one to oil him up for his photos, or adjust his fucking Calvin Kleins—and I don't mean jeans.

Me: Yeah. Just don't be disappointed if he's kind of an ass.

BB: It's all good, Lexi. I can handle it.

She's probably right, but I still hate this. And damn it, I can't let on that I know. She's going out of town to interview this jackass male model, I know about it, and I can't say a word.

I have never gotten this territorial over a woman before. Not once in my life. But I don't care that this relationship is new. Mia has awakened something primal inside me, a fierce desire to claim her. To own every inch of that woman. To leave my scent on her so any asshole who comes near won't dare so much as *look* in her direction.

Whether or not she tells me about the interview doesn't matter. There's only one thing a man can do when faced with a situation like this.

I have to make sure this woman knows good and well that

She's.

Fucking.

Mine.

19

MIA

The smoldering look Alex gives me when he picks me up sends a cascade of sensations thrumming through my entire body. A shiver races down my spine. My lips tingle. Heat surges through my core, leaving me to wonder if I'm going to need to change my panties before we leave.

It's just a look—a subtle narrowing of his brown eyes, a serious furrow to his brow. His chiseled jaw set in a hard line. His eyes devour me. I know, in the depths of my soul, that he's thinking very dirty thoughts right now. I don't know why. I don't know what brought this on. But I feel like prey being sized up by a much larger, much faster, much scarier predator.

I fucking love it.

Despite my sister's warnings to keep my feet on the ground, I've been floating in the clouds pretty much nonstop. I see Alex almost every day, and I never try to keep any distance between us. There's a piece of me that wonders if I should be holding back. Keeping a bit of myself separate from him. Should I make sure we aren't walking on the edge of a cliff before I go all-in? Or should I give in to what is turning into a crazy whirlwind romance, the likes of which I didn't think existed outside of my favorite books?

The way he's looking at me now leaves me no choice but to give in.

Although truthfully, I don't really want the choice.

One side of his mouth curls up, ever so slightly, in the barest hint of a smile. The intensity never leaves his eyes, and when he speaks, his voice is rich and deep, flowing over me like warm honey. "Hi, beautiful."

Oh. My. God.

I can feel the vibration of his words in my chest and I want to melt into a puddle at his feet.

"Hi." That's all I manage to say, but I guess that's what happens when your brain is suddenly short circuiting.

"Ready?" he asks.

With a deep breath to hopefully clear my head, I nod. He helps me into my coat and pulls my hair out from under it. His hands linger near my neck, trailing through my thick tresses, and his touch sends another flurry of sparks through me.

I don't know if I'm going to make it through dinner if he keeps doing this.

We head to the restaurant and wait while the host sees to our table. Alex slides his hand into mine and rubs my thumb, standing close enough that I can feel the heat of his body. I glance up at his face and the look he gives me is positively *obscene*. His tongue wets his lips, his eyes are fierce, and he leans in to kiss my forehead. A forehead kiss is usually a sweet gesture. This is *not* sweet. This is possessive and passionate, like he's leaving a mark on me for everyone to see.

By the time we're shown to our table, my heart is racing, my panties are soaked, and my cheeks are warm. We order wine, and dinner—although ten seconds after the waiter leaves, I can't remember what I'm having. Alex never takes his eyes off me. Not when the waiter takes his order. Not when our food arrives. We talk, like usual, but there's a deep undercurrent of desire in his voice. My mind is so preoccupied with the throbbing between my legs, it's hard to keep up with the conversation. Amazingly, I don't drop anything, or spill my wine. The strange thing is, I'm not flustered. My hands and feet feel like they're connected to my body, instead of flailing around independently. I'm completely comfortable—but so fucking aroused I can barely stand it.

The waiter approaches our table after our plates have been cleared. "Can I interest you in dessert?"

Alex's eyes don't leave mine. "No, thank you. I'll be having something else for dessert tonight."

I swallow hard, my eyes widening.

The waiter clears his throat and gives Alex the check. Without looking at the waiter, Alex pulls out a credit card and hands it over.

"What is going on with you tonight?" I ask, my voice low.

He raises his eyebrows. "What do you mean?"

I look him up and down. His posture is relaxed, assured. His eyes haven't once lost their burning intensity. He has the look of a man who knows exactly what he wants, and is completely confident he's going to get it.

He should be. He's absolutely going to get it. Whatever he wants, I'm giving it to him.

"I don't know, you're just very intense tonight," I say.

His lips turn up in a smile. "Is that a bad thing?"

"No."

"Good." He leans forward and takes my hand, then brings it up to his lips. He kisses the backs of my fingers. I shiver, my body turning to liquid at the feel of his mouth on my hand. "I'm just enjoying you, and I want you to know that."

I almost swoon right out of my chair. Luckily, Alex is still holding my hand. "Thanks. I'm enjoying you too."

"That's good to hear," he says. God, that voice. So low and melodic. "My place?"

"Yes," I breathe. "Now, please."

The waiter comes back and as soon as Alex signs the check, I'm ready to grab my things and dash out the door. But Alex stands and helps me into my coat, completely unhurried. He puts on his own coat, gives me another ridiculously sexy smile, and leads me out to his car.

He puts his hand on my thigh while he drives us to his apartment. I tilt my legs apart and glance at him from the corner of my eye. His lips twitch in a small smile. Without taking his eyes off the road, he runs his hand higher up my leg and slips it beneath my skirt. He keeps going, and I gasp a little as he reaches the edge of my panties. One finger slides against the crease of my thigh. I open my legs more, my breath coming faster. His fingers slide across my underwear and he gently caresses my clit. The soft touch is like a hitting a button that sets me on fire. My eyes flutter and my hand darts out to stabilize myself against the door.

"Holy shit."

"Mm, baby, your panties are so wet," he says.

I lean my head against the back rest and tilt my face so I can look at him. "I've been wet for you all night."

His jaw clenches and he practically growls. He pushes my panties to the side and slides his fingers along the outside of my slit. I spare half a thought for whether people can see in the windows of his car. But that worry fizzles into nothing as he dips his fingertips into my pussy and presses against my clit.

He plays with me, his fingers teasing, sliding, and caressing while he drives. My eyes roll back and I let the flood of pleasure wash over me.

"We better be close to your place, or I'm going to make you pull over and fuck me in this car," I say.

As if in answer, he pushes his fingers in deeper. I moan and grab his arm.

He pulls his hand away and I watch as he puts his fingers in his mouth and licks my wetness off them. His eyes close for a second and he groans. "I can't fucking wait to taste you."

He parks and thankfully I remember to pull my skirt down before I get out. My heart thunders, my nipples tingle, and don't even get me started on the party going on between my legs. It's not just a party; it's a fucking rave.

Unfortunately—or fortunately, depending on how you look at it—we aren't alone in the elevator when we head up to his floor. I think if we *were* alone we'd do something to get ourselves arrested, so I suppose it's better this way. But there's a haze over my vision and my mind is completely clouded with lust. Alex reaches under my wool coat, splays his hand across my ass, and squeezes—hard. My eyes widen and I suck in a breath. The two men sharing the elevator glance in my direction. Alex doesn't pay attention to them. He leans over and rubs his slightly scratchy, slightly soft, so fucking sexy bearded jaw from my temple down my cheek.

I swallow hard and lift my eyes in a silent plea that this elevator will not choose this moment to get stuck.

The doors open and Alex ushers me out. He keeps his hand shamelessly on my ass and I can feel the other men's eyes on us as we leave.

Not like I care. All I can think about is keeping my legs moving in a forward direction so we can get behind a fucking closed door. Now.

We make it to his apartment and he shuts the door behind me. I put my purse down and he helps me take off my coat, tossing it onto the couch. He takes off his own coat, deliberately, one arm at a time, and hangs it on the back of a chair. Then he loosens the collar of his button-down shirt and turns his white-hot gaze back on me.

"On the bed. Naked. Now."

Sir, yes sir. I bite my lip and walk past him. He doesn't touch me, just watches me go. I wait until I get into his bedroom to start stripping. He doesn't follow me in right away, but I don't dream of disobeying him. I take off my clothes, leaving everything on the floor, set my glasses on the nightstand, and get on the bed.

He appears in the doorway a moment later with glass of Scotch in his hand. He leans against the door frame, his eyes devouring me, and takes a sip.

I stare right back. My nipples are hard, my pussy throbbing, and I'm about ready to start touching myself just to get things started.

Maybe he wants me to. Maybe he likes to watch.

Holding his gaze, I trail my fingers down between my breasts, past my belly button, and toward my center. His jaw tightens and he swallows hard, sending his Adam's apple bobbing in his throat. I tip my knees open and his eyes narrow. Then I slide my fingers down, feeling my soft skin, and rub my swollen clit.

Alex growls again, the noise deep and primal.

Feeling like I'm acting out a scene from a novel I've read— and maybe I am, this seems familiar—I ease into the feel of my fingers swirling around my sensitive nerves. My legs widen and I slide my fingers inside my pussy to get them wet, then rub myself just the way I like it. Alex walks over to the bed, sets his drink on the nightstand with a clink, and starts unbuttoning his shirt. I don't stop, my breath quickening as I touch myself. I've never done this in front of someone before, but watching him watch me is incredibly erotic.

His eyes don't leave my pussy as he slowly unfastens each button, revealing his broad chest and chiseled abs. He lets his shirt fall to the floor, then takes off his pants and underwear. I stare at his thick cock, the sight of it heating me up even more.

He picks up his drink and sits on the edge of the bed. Licking his lips, he plucks an ice cube from his glass and touches it to my belly. I gasp and move my hand, but keep my legs spread open. He slides the ice cube down, leaving a trail of moisture on my skin, until he gets to my pussy. I gasp as he runs it along the outside, the cold biting. He lets it slip inside me, then pulls it out again and drops it back into his glass. It clinks against the other ice cubes and he lifts it to his mouth to take another sip.

Holy shit.

"Now that I've had a taste of you, I need more," he says.

He grabs my hips and turns me, pulling my ass to the edge of the bed. His jaw grazes the inside of my thigh. I'm afraid I'm going to come the second his tongue touches me, but he seems to know I need him to take control of my body. He licks me with the tip of his tongue, once on each side of my opening. The sensation both lights me up and calms me down.

With slow, sensual strokes, he explores me. I close my eyes and lose myself in the warm wetness of his tongue. He swirls it around my clit, teasing me.

Suddenly, he dives in harder, pushing his tongue into my pussy and dragging it out again. His rhythm is electrifying, the feel of his mouth absolute bliss. I shudder and moan as he moves. He licks and sucks and growls into me, his beard stimulating my sensitive skin.

"Oh fuck... Alex... yes..."

I thread my hands through his hair and he lifts his eyes to meet mine. Our gazes lock and he groans again. He slides two fingers into my pussy while his mouth concentrates on my clit. I throw my head back and call out, bucking my hips against his face. His hand digs into my thigh, his mouth vibrates, and his tongue dances across my clit.

The tension builds, heat rushing to my core. I moan and call his name. I'm on fucking fire, my pussy tightening with a sensation I've never felt before.

With a rush of pleasure that constricts my throat and sends all thoughts fleeing, I explode. I claw at the sheets, arch my back, and ride the wave as it sweeps me away. Alex doesn't stop, and as my orgasm peaks and starts to fade, it climbs and I burst all over again. I completely lose control, moaning and writhing while this man absolutely annihilates me.

The orgasm—or orgasms, as in multiple, thank you very much—subside. I lay on the bed, panting, trying to catch my breath. Alex kisses and licks and nibbles my thighs while I recover.

"God, Alex, I can't even think right now," I say between breaths.

He grabs my hips and flips me over onto my belly, then slides his hand up my spine and fists it through my hair. He grabs it at the base of my neck and pulls so my head lifts off the bed.

"Baby," he says, his voice rough, "I'm just getting started."

20

ALEX

I keep hold of Mia's hair, just tight enough that she's in my control. She looks at me over her shoulder, her eyes still glassy, and bites her lower lip.

I lean over her and kiss the back of her neck, letting my cock dig into her ass. She shudders, and I rub against her, enjoying her bare skin against my dick. The feel of her body and the taste of her in my mouth are making me crazy.

"Don't move." I get a condom from the nightstand and roll it on.

Mia stays poised over the edge of the bed, bent at the waist. I grab her hips and slide into her from behind. She moans as she takes my full length. I pause, enjoying the feel of her pussy wrapped around me. She arches her back and pushes against me, like she's trying to get me in deeper.

I hold tight to her hips and move in and out. This view is phenomenal. Her hair spilling down her back. Her narrow waist. The curve of her hips. Her ass. Fuck, *that ass*.

"God, Mia, you're so fucking sexy."

I pick up the pace and she moans with every thrust. I want to imprint her senses with the feel of our bodies together. I want her to remember how my cock feels even when I'm not inside her. I want her to crave me. Want me. Only me.

I want her to know she's mine.

I pull out and flip her over. She crawls back onto the bed and I climb on top of her. I kiss her as I sink into her again, letting the taste of her pass between us. Her tongue dances with mine and our bodies move. God, she's so good. I drive my hips, plunging my cock into her.

"Holy shit," she breathes.

She runs her soft hands all over my skin, caressing my chest, running her fingers along my jaw, through my hair. Our eyes meet and I pause, my cock buried deep inside her. I stare into her eyes for a long moment, drinking in the sight of her.

I'm hit with something I've never felt before. All my nerves lighting up, firing at once. Our bodies sliding together, my cock surrounded by her heat. Her breath on my skin. Her scent filling me. But there's more. There's a feeling deep in my chest. An ache. A longing. I know in this moment, I'm exactly where I'm meant to be. My body locked with hers, connected in the most intimate way possible.

I kiss her, savoring the feel of our mouths tangled together. She moves her hips and I thrust again, easily sliding through her wetness. The rest of the world goes dark. There's nothing else that matters.

"I love the way you fuck me," she says.

"Does that feel good?"

Her eyes roll back. "So amazing."

I cup her breast and lick the delicate nub of her nipple. I put my mouth around it and suck, gently at first. Mia responds and I keep thrusting. I suck harder and she cries out, arching her back. I guide her hand to her breast and she squeezes it while I suck the other one. I love watching her touch herself. She flicks her fingers over her nipple and I graze the other with my teeth.

Moving her hand, I turn my attention to her other breast, licking and sucking while she writhes beneath me. Her skin tastes like heaven and the feel of her tits in my mouth is unreal.

"Please make me come, Alex," she says, her voice breathy and urgent. "You're driving me insane."

"I will, baby. I'll give you everything you need."

She bucks her hips and digs her fingers into my back, but I slow down. I won't let her set the pace. I brace myself on top of her and plunge in and out with slow, deliberate strokes.

I lean into her, our lips brushing together, and speak in a low growl. "This pussy is mine, you hear me?"

"All yours."

I grab her ass and thrust into her again. "This ass is mine."

"Yours."

I suck her nipple—hard—and it pops out of my mouth. "These tits are mine."

"Yours, baby," she says, almost breathless.

I drive into her and hold there, as deep as I can go, bottoming out. "You're mine, Mia."

She lifts her arms over her head and closes her eyes, surrendering to me fully. "Alex, I'm yours."

I hook my arm beneath her leg, pulling it higher, and fuck her as hard and as deep as I can. She loses control, moving with me, calling out. The heat in her pussy builds, the pressure so sweet.

Tension intensifies to a breaking point. I drive my hips, plunging in, grinding against her. She starts coming, her pussy clenched tight, pulsing around my cock. I give her what she needs, thrusting while she cries out.

"Yes... oh... yes... Alex..."

I give in. I lose myself in all of it—in her, in us, in this moment. And I fucking detonate.

Pressure breaks through me, surging as my balls unleash,

and I come hard. Every muscle in my body contracts as I unload in her. I groan into her neck with every pulse, the waves of pleasure rolling through me. I'm undone.

I take ragged breaths, my mind blank. I'm high as fuck, saturated by the way she feels, the way she smells, the way she tastes. Her arms wrap around me, her skin hot and sticky against mine. My heart knocks against my ribs and my body is spent.

I roll off her, but I'm not ready to let go. I quickly tie off the condom—I'll deal with it later—and gather her in my arms. We lie together in silence while we both catch our breath. She tucks her toes between my feet and nestles her cheek against my chest. I kiss the top of her head and hold her close.

Her fingers trace little circles on my skin. I kiss her head again and she tilts her face up to look at me. "Oh my god, Alex, I think I love you."

We both freeze. Her eyes widen, and I know she just spoke without thinking. She could have been kidding—an off-hand comment meant to be funny that winds up awkward. That would be just like Mia.

But I can tell by the expression on her face, it wasn't a joke.

"Sorry... that was... no filter... I mean..." She stumbles over her words, pulling away from me. Usually she recovers, and finishes with what she wants to say. This time she opens her mouth again, but can't seem to find the words.

My eyes don't leave hers. Hearing her say that, however spontaneous, doesn't freak me out. In fact, I loved hearing her say it. She fills something inside me I didn't realize was empty. I look into her bright blue eyes and my heart races, adrenaline flooding my system.

I reach out and pull her to me, drawing her mouth to mine. I savor her sweet lips and let what I'm about to say settle in my mind.

"I think I love you too."

"Oh," she says. "I just blurted that out and now you said it. Are we saying this?"

"Do you want me to say it again?"

"I think maybe yes," she says.

I laugh softly. "Mia, I'm in love with you."

"I was trying to figure out how to back out of that," she says. "But I wasn't kidding. I am *so* in love with you."

Our mouths connect, and we kiss and laugh and kiss more. I pull the covers over us and we settle in, our arms and legs wound together, our bodies as close as we can be without lying on top of each other. I hold her against me and close my eyes. I fall asleep with her scent in my nose, her skin against mine.

There's nowhere I'd rather be.

21

ALEX

*M*ia smiles at me from her table when I walk in the door. It's been a few days since we've seen each other, so I came down to meet her for lunch at a cafe near her office. Seeing her, even from across a crowded restaurant, eases the mild ache I've been living with. Damn, I missed her.

I walk over to her table and she stands.

"Hi, beautiful." I lean down and kiss her softly.

She laughs a little and adjusts her glasses. "Hey."

We both take our seats and a waitress comes with two cups of coffee.

"I ordered us both coffee," she says. "I hope you don't mind."

"Not at all," I say. "Thanks. How have you been?"

She shrugs. "Busy. I have a lot to get done this week, so I've been working late."

"Yeah, I know what you mean. This has been a crazy week for me too." It's always a little tricky to talk to Mia about my job without revealing any details. But this week has been nuts. I'm trying to finish up a new book, and Kendra and I are busy coordinating the details of a huge giveaway.

"I'm glad you suggested lunch," she says. "I've missed you."

"I've missed you too. What do you have going on tomorrow? If you're tired, we can stay in and watch a movie."

I actually know what she has going on tomorrow. She's going to Portland to interview Antonio Zane. Maybe it's a dick move to prod her about it, but I wonder what she's going to say.

"Oh, I can't. I have to go out of town. For work."

"That's too bad," I say. "How long will you be gone?"

"Just the day, but I'm not sure when I'll be back. Probably late." She takes a deep breath and looks down at her cup. "Actually, that's not true. It isn't for work."

Oh shit. Is she going to tell me?

"I'm going down to Portland to interview someone," she says. "I know I've never mentioned it, but I run a romance book blog. It started out as just book reviews, but it's grown a lot. I feature new books and authors, industry news, all kinds of things. Anyway, I wrote to this book cover model on a whim; I never thought he'd answer. But he did. He has a photo shoot and he invited me to come. I jumped at the chance."

Yep, she's telling me. "Wow, that sounds like a great opportunity."

"Yeah, it is," she says. "I'm sorry I didn't just say what was going on. The thing is, I've never told anyone about my blog before. I use a pseudonym, so I'm anonymous online. And I keep that whole side of myself separate from me as Mia. Maybe I shouldn't be so secretive about it, but I am."

"Why are you secretive about it?"

"Safety for one," she says. "I know the chance of some author coming after me for a bad review is slim, but people are crazy. And my family would never understand the time I put into it. They'd tell me to work on something productive. It's just always seemed easier to keep it hidden from the people I know in real life. People already give me a hard time for being such a bookworm. This would make it worse."

"That sucks about your family," I say, trying to keep my tone casual. But I'm freaking out a little. She's telling me she's BB. Maybe I should tell her I'm Lexi.

Although having a blog, and being a man with a female pen name aren't exactly the same thing.

And then there's the whole *we know each other already* part.

Shit.

"Yeah, but I'm used to it. And, I don't know, there's something freeing about being anonymous. I feel like I can be myself in a way I can't in person. I'm much more comfortable behind the safety of a computer screen, so I don't mess things up as much. I don't blurt out stupid things and if I knock something over, no one can see it."

I reach out and run my fingers over the back of her hand. "I don't think you blurt out stupid things."

She laughs. "Have you met me? I do it all the time."

"No, you're honest," I say. "I've known so many women who never say what they're thinking. I love hearing what's really on your mind."

"Okay, I need to know what's wrong with you," she says.

I blink at her. "What?"

She puts a hand to her forehead. "No, I mean... Sorry... I did it again, see?" She takes a deep breath. "You're just insanely perfect. I keep waiting for the catch."

"I'm not even close to perfect," I say.

"You're really close, actually," she says. "You're right out of a book. Gorgeous and sexy. Romantic. Fun. I joked for years that all my book boyfriends ruined me for real men, but you give those fictional guys a run for their money."

I take a sip of my coffee to give myself a second to think. *There's a big catch, Mia, and it's that I've been lying to you about who I am.*

I'm at war with myself over what to say. This is all happening so fast. Not just this conversation—all of it. I thought it would be months before I'd even *consider* telling Mia about Lexi.

Maybe I'm getting swept up in this too quickly. But I'm not used to dealing with so much fucking emotion. I've never felt this way about anyone before. Not my first girlfriend in high school. Not Janine, whom I *married*.

But Mia came out of nowhere and nothing has been the same since we met. I'm consumed by her. I think about her all the time. I want to spend every waking moment with her. And that's crazy. This kind of thing doesn't happen in real life. Sure, it happens in books. I've written about insta-love. It always seemed so unrealistic. Fun to write about, but not at all real.

Except I'm looking at Mia and I'm feeling a hundred things at once. I want to touch her. I want to drag her into the back and kiss her until we're both breathless. I want to stay up all night worshiping her body. Talking and laughing with her.

I'm fucking in love with this woman.

I have to tell her about Lexi. But suddenly I'm filled with the fear that she's going to be angry. What if she doesn't forgive me?

"I'm sorry," she says. "I'm sitting here gushing over you and making you uncomfortable."

"No, you aren't." I take a deep breath. I just have to put it out there and hope I can explain. Hope she'll understand. "Mia—"

Her phone rings and she gasps. "Oh, shit. Who's calling me? No one calls me." She picks it up and looks at the screen, her eyes widening. "Oh my god, it's Shelby. That probably means... Hello? Shelby? Yes. Now? Okay. Is Daniel there? Good. Don't worry. I'm on my way."

Mia hangs up and grabs her purse. "Alex, I am so sorry. Shelby's in labor. She should have had a few more weeks, I wasn't expecting this. She needs me to come get Alanna so she can go to the hospital."

"Yeah, of course." *Shit.* "Do you want me to drive you or

anything?"

"No, I'm good," she says, pushing her glasses up her nose. "I'm sorry, I just need to hurry. I'll text you when things calm down, okay?"

I stand and wrap her in my arms. "Yeah, of course. Tell Shelby congratulations."

"I will."

She lifts up on her toes to kiss me and seconds later, I'm watching her back as she hurries out the door.

Well, that didn't go very well.

I don't have any reason to stay, so I leave some money on the table and head home. I pick up lunch on the way, and try to get some work done. I'm worried about Mia, but hours go by and I don't hear from her. I resist the urge to text her. She's busy with her family stuff; she doesn't need me getting all weird and possessive by texting her constantly.

I look up at the clock and realize it's after eight. I got so caught up in writing, I forgot to stop for dinner. I'm about to scrounge up something to eat, when I hear the ding of a message notification on my laptop.

BB: Hey Lexi. Are you busy?

Me: No more than usual. What's up?

BB: This has been the craziest day. I was out with my boyfriend (also, wow, I think that's the first time I've called him that), and I got the call that my sister was in labor. I raced up to her house to stay with my niece while she went to the hospital. But something went wrong. The baby is okay, but they had to do an emergency C-section. That should have been fine, but I guess my sister was still bleeding or something, and they had to take her back in for another surgery. I don't know what's going on. My niece is in bed, so I can't leave, and no one is answering my texts. I'm kind of freaking out.

Me: Holy shit. That's really scary.

BB: I know. I'm so worried about her.

I pause, not sure what else to say. Why hasn't Mia texted me to tell me what's going on? She goes to Lexi first? What's that about?

I pick up my phone and press the button. Nothing happens; the screen stays dark. I hold it down longer. Still nothing. Son of a bitch, my battery died. I plug it in and try to turn it on again. The screen lights up and the message notification blinks. Mia did try to text me. Several times. Damn it. I send her one last quick message from my laptop as Lexi.

Me: I hope you hear from them soon, BB. And I hope your sister is okay.

BB: Thanks. It's just so crazy. I tried to text my boyfriend, but he isn't responding.

Fuck. I grab my phone and the stupid charger comes loose. My battery is at one percent. *Don't fucking die again, you piece of shit.* I plug it back in, holding it carefully so the charger won't disconnect again, and send her a text.

Me: I'm so sorry, baby. My phone died and I just realized. Have you heard anything?

Mia: There you are! Actually I just got a text from my brother-in-law two seconds ago. She's out of surgery. Looks like she'll be okay. Baby is healthy.

Me: So glad to hear that. Do you want me to come up?

Mia: That's so sweet, but it's okay. I'm just going to read until I fall asleep. Alanna wakes up at like 5, so...

Me: If you're sure.

Mia: Yeah. What are you doing tomorrow?

Me: Nothing planned. Can I come see you?

Mia: Yeah, if you don't mind hanging out with the little pirate princess.

Me: Not at all. I'd love to meet her.

Mia: You're amazing. I'll text you tomorrow then.

Me: Perfect. Miss you.

Mia: Miss you too. And... love you.

I can't stop the grin that steals over my face.

Me: I love you too, baby.

I blow out a breath as I put down my phone. I hate having this Lexi thing hanging over our heads. But I can't tell her tomorrow while she's babysitting her niece. Especially after dealing with the stress of everything with her sister.

My phone dings with another text, but it's Kendra.

Kendra: Did you get the books for the giveaway?

Me: Yeah, they came today.

Kendra: I hope you've been doing your hand yoga.

Me: WTF Kendra. I'm with Mia now, I don't need to exercise my hand.

Kendra: You're so disgusting. I mean because you have to sign them all.

Me: Sign them? That's going to look weird. I don't have girl handwriting.

Kendra: Who cares. Just make it look cute.

Me: Cute? How do I make a signature cute?

Kendra: I don't know. Put a little heart above the i in Lexi.

Me: Seriously?

Kendra: Why not? That's totes adorbs.

Me: Did you really just say totes adorbs? Come over and sign these. I'm not doing it.

Kendra: How much will you pay me?

Me: I'll order you fifty bucks worth of Godiva right now.

Kendra: Done. I'll be there in twenty.

I chuckle to myself as I bring up the Godiva website. I'll definitely pay Kendra in chocolate to sign these books for me.

As for Mia, the more I think about it, the more certain I am that I can't tell her about Lexi tomorrow. I'll wait until we have some time alone. I guess a few more days won't make a difference anyway.

22

MIA

My sister's bleary-eyed existence makes a lot more sense after being awoken by a four-year-old bundle of energy at five fifteen. I'm not ashamed to admit, I doze on the couch while she watches cartoons for the next few hours. For all I know, the poor kid is going to have brain damage from the amount of TV I'm letting her watch. But come on. Five fifteen? That barely qualifies as morning.

I'm a little bummed at missing the interview today. I sent Antonio an email late last night, explaining what happened. He responded with a short *maybe another time*. I'm not sure if I'll get another chance, but such is life.

Around eight, my brother-in-law calls. Shelby is doing well enough for visitors, so we can come down to the hospital to see Alanna's new baby brother. When we get there, I hold him first, cradling the soft bundle of tiny sleeping human. I scowl at Shelby when she insists I sit down when I'm holding him—it's not like I'd drop him.

They named him Daniel Junior. I immediately start calling him DJ, but Shelby tells me in no uncertain terms that this child will not be referred to by his initials. While I sit with Alanna to help her hold her new brother, I hear Shelby and Daniel talking in hushed whispers about whether they should rethink the baby's name.

Alanna gets restless after a while, so I take her home. It's nearly lunchtime, so I send Alex a text.

Me: Hey. Shelby is doing better. Got to hold the baby. He's cute. Plans today?

Alex: Actually, Caleb just called. He needs someone to watch my niece, so I guess I'm babysitting too.

Me: Isn't she about four? We should get them together. The small humans can play!

Alex: And the big humans?

Me: We'll see what we can get away with.

Alex: Sounds great. They're staying with my dad, so I'm heading over there in half an hour. Should I come to you?

Me: Either way.

Alex: Wait, do four-year-olds need car seats or something?

Me: Never mind. I'll come to you. Text me your dad's address and I'll meet you there.

About an hour later, we pull up to a dark red rambler with white trim. Alex's car is out front and I park behind him. Alanna runs toward the front door, leaving a trail of sparkly enthusiasm behind her. I let her knock, and a woman with shoulder-length brown hair and eyes just like Alex opens the door.

"Oh, hi," I say, suddenly flustered. *Oh my god, his sister.*

Her face breaks into a wide smile. "Hi, you must be Mia." She holds out her hand. "I'm Kendra. It is so nice to finally meet you."

I take her hand. *Be cool, Mia. Don't say anything stupid.* "Wow, you look just like Alex. I don't mean you look like a guy. You're very feminine. But you have the same eyes. They're very pretty. Not that Alex has pretty eyes, necessarily. Maybe pretty isn't the right word." I stop myself before I keep rambling and make this worse. I close my eyes for a second and take a breath. "Sorry, I'll start over. Hi, it's nice to meet you too."

She smiles and drops my hand. God, I held it way too long. She steps aside so Alanna and I can come in, but my toe catches on the threshold and I stumble in through the door. I right myself before I crash into Kendra, but it's close.

"Sorry," I say.

"There she is," Alex says as he walks toward the door. "Kendra, I thought you left ten minutes ago. Did you overhear my conversation with Dad and covertly stay so you could meet Mia?"

"Of course," she says, her tone matter-of-fact.

Alex shakes his head. "All right, well, Mia, this is Kendra. Kendra, this is Mia."

"We did that part already, Alex, catch up," Kendra says. "Although I do have to go. But it is so nice to meet you, Mia. Hopefully I'll see you again soon."

"Yeah, that would be great," I say.

Kendra raises her eyebrows and gives Alex a not-at-all concealed thumbs up before heading out the front door.

A little girl with dark brown hair, who looks to be about Alanna's age, peeks around a corner.

"Come here, Charlotte," Alex says, his voice light and soothing. "It's okay. This is Alanna."

Alanna bounces up on her tiptoes a few times.

I grab her hand so she doesn't run and tackle Charlotte. "Slow down, kiddo."

Alex goes back to Charlotte and picks her up. She wraps her arms around him and buries her face in his neck. "Charlotte is a little shy at first, especially since her daddy isn't here."

It takes Alex a minute or two to coax Charlotte into saying hi to Alanna. But once she peels herself away from him, Alanna's friendliness takes over. In minutes, she's holding hands with Charlotte while they walk into another room to play.

"Wow, she's good," Alex says. "It took me an entire day to get Charlotte to warm up to me."

"Yeah, Alanna is a social butterfly," I say.

He steps closer and slides his hands around my waist, drawing me into him. I tilt my face up and he kisses me with a lot more eagerness than I was expecting, considering we're standing in the middle of his dad's house.

"Hey," he says quietly when he pulls away.

I feel a bit wobbly and I lean into him so I don't trip again. "Hey."

"I'm glad this worked out."

"Me too," I say. "The girls will have fun."

Alex smiles and I get a rush of tingles. It's all I can do not to giggle.

A voice comes from the other room. "Alex, is that nice young lady here yet?"

"Yeah, Dad, just a second," he says. "Do you mind saying hi to my dad?"

"Of course not."

He grabs my hand, twining his fingers with mine, and leads me into the family room. His dad is sitting in a reclining chair facing a TV. He lowers a newspaper and smiles at me. Alex is the spitting image of his father, only younger. Same eyes, same sweet smile. His dad has a pair of reading glasses perched on his nose and his hair is mostly gray.

"Hello again," he says. "It's nice to see you."

"You too, Mr. Lawson," I say.

"Call me Ken," he says with a wave of his hand.

"How are you feeling?" I ask. "Ready for Dr. Lander to cut you open?"

Ken smiles. "Believe it or not, I am. Anxious to get this over with."

"I believe it," I say. "Dr. Lander is the best. His bedside manner is awful, but he's an amazing surgeon."

"Cocky son of a bitch, isn't he?" Ken says.

"Dad," Alex says.

"No, it's true," I say. "Lander *is* a cocky son of a bitch. But he's the best at what he does. You wouldn't want anyone else. If he's being a jerk when you're awake, just tell his nurse. She'll kick his ass."

"I'll do that," Ken says. He turns to Alex. "I like her."

Alex runs his hand up and down my back. "Me too."

Ken picks up his newspaper, the black and white newsprint crinkling as he straightens it. "Well, I won't keep you. I know you're keeping an eye on my granddaughter."

Alex leads me into the other room. There's a couch and two armchairs facing a fireplace, and a dark coffee table. We sit, Alex pulling me down so I'm almost on top of him. He touches my chin and brings me in for a kiss. His scruff brushes my face and his lips press against mine. He pulls me closer, his hand sliding behind my head, his fingers threading through my hair.

I half-listen for the sound of four-year-old girl feet. And I'm pretty sure we'd hear Alex's dad if he got up. I feel a little bit like a naughty teenager, making out one room away from my boyfriend's dad. And if Alanna catches us, I know she'll blab to Shelby about it.

But when Alex kisses me like this, it's really hard to care about anything else.

"Auntie Mia?"

Alanna's voice startles me and I pull away from Alex. I bite my lip and swallow hard, willing myself not to blush.

"Hey, kiddo," I say. "What's up?"

She and Charlotte stand in the hallway, staring at us with open mouths.

Oops.

"Are you married?" Alanna asks.

"Um, no," I say. "Why?"

"Because sometimes Mommy and Daddy kiss, and when I said I wanted to kiss Billy Jones at preschool, Mommy said that's something only married people do."

My eyes widen and now I'm sure I'm getting flushed. "Well, Alanna... That's just... I mean... It's not..."

"Sometimes when two grown-ups are in love, they like to kiss each other," Alex says, his voice smooth as glass.

"And you love Auntie Mia?" Alanna asks.

"Yep," he says.

"Okay," Alanna says. "Want to play tea party?"

I let out a breath, my shoulders slumping, and mouth a quick *thank you* to Alex.

"Sure, we'd love to play tea party," he says.

Charlotte comes over and climbs in Alex's lap. Alanna brings a pink plastic tea set. She wedges herself between me and Alex and starts passing out tea cups.

The girls seem much more interested in playing tea party with Alex than with me, so I scoot over a little to give them space, and watch. Charlotte tucks her legs up and leans against him, clutching her teacup in delicate fingers. Alanna does most of the talking, telling an elaborate story about how they are princesses and Alex is the king. Alex laughs and holds his tiny teacup with his pinky outstretched, then pretends to take a sip.

It's absolutely one of the sweetest things I've ever seen in my entire life. This gorgeous man with his hot as sin body and smile that takes my breath away, sitting on a couch with two little girls snuggling up against him, pretending to drink tea from plastic cups.

It's a little bit frightening how fucking turned on I am.

Then Alex meets my eyes and winks. I think I might die.

When the girls tire of playing with the tea set, they disappear for a few minutes and return with teddy bears. They cuddle against Alex again, playing with the bears in his lap. He smiles and shakes his head while they play on him as if he's part of the furniture.

All I can do is stare.

I try not to. I don't want to act like a crazy person. But I'm overcome. I literally ran into him by random chance, and every day since has been like a waking dream. He's everything. No writer could have come close to creating a hero so perfect for me. There's a voice inside my head that still keeps trying to remind me that this is moving fast. That I've fallen head over heels in love with him and maybe I should slow it down.

But I'm completely in his power. His smile makes me giddy, his kiss melts me. His touch sets me on fire.

And seeing him with these adorable little girls, I can't help but imagine the future. A future with him in it, and maybe even a little girl or boy of our own.

I swallow hard so I don't tear up. Holy shit, this is crazy. He meets my eyes and I grin at him with a smile that's too big. But I don't care. The last bits of hesitation I've been feeling fall away. I'm crazy in love with him. End of story.

After the girls play for a while, we let them watch TV. I join Alex in the kitchen to throw together some dinner for all of us. His brother Caleb arrives while we're cooking, and Kendra comes back shortly after. All the Lawson kids favor their father, and look strikingly alike. Caleb is tall and fit with the same deep brown eyes and a pleasant smile.

Alanna and I eat dinner with Alex and his family, and I'm filled with a sense of contentment. My awkwardness is nowhere to be seen. No spills, no feeling tongue-tied.

I actually feel like I belong.

As much as I don't want this day to end, after dinner I tear Alanna away from her new best friend and take her home. I tuck her into bed, send Shelby a text to see how she's doing, and plop down on the couch with my laptop.

What an amazing day. I *have* to tell Lexi.

Me: OMG, Lexi, send help. My ovaries are literally exploding.

Lexi: Um... are you okay?

Me: Yeah. I visited my sister and got to hold her new baby. It's a boy, and he's so tiny and cute. But that wasn't what did it. I was babysitting my niece all day, and my boyfriend was babysitting his niece. So we got them together. Words cannot express how adorable he was with them. I melted into a big pool of nonsensical mush.

Lexi: That's so cute.

Me: Oh it was. I've never felt that urge before. I always figured I'd have kids someday—emphasis on the someday part. But that man made my ovaries positively ache. Don't tell him, though, LOL. I wouldn't want to freak him out by telling him I have mad baby fever.

Lexi: Wow, baby fever? You guys haven't been together that long, have you?

Me: No. I'm not saying I'm going to poke holes in his condoms or anything. But I could really see it with him, you know? I was watching him sit with those little girls and I had this vision of the two of us, in the future. With kids. And it felt really good.

Lexi doesn't answer and I wonder if she had to go offline abruptly. I put my phone down and lie back against the couch cushions. After getting up so early this morning, I'm exhausted. I pull a throw blanket over me and curl up. Shelby has a guest room upstairs, but I might just sleep here tonight. I'm suddenly too tired to care, and I know Alanna's going to be up well before I'm ready for her.

23

ALEX

I exit out of messenger. I didn't even respond to her last message. But what the fuck am I supposed to say to that? Poke holes in my condoms? Baby fever? Ovaries exploding?

Holy shit. Did I just find out my girlfriend is baby crazy?

Although, I think what she's saying is that she can see that with me. Not that she necessarily wants it *now*.

That's an alarming revelation in its own way. But what's even more alarming is that I can see it too. I can see it all. Mia and I together... married... children.

Holy shit. Again.

Kendra went home already, but Caleb comes out after putting Charlotte to bed. He hands me a beer and sits down in the chair next to me.

"Thanks again for watching her today," he says. "That was a big help."

"It was no problem," I say. "She's a sweet kid."

He smiles. "She sure is."

"Can I ask you something?"

"Sure." He opens his beer and reaches over with the bottle opener to do mine. It hisses as the cap comes off.

"Did you and Melanie plan to have Charlotte when you did?" I ask.

"To be honest, no," he says. "We thought we'd wait a while longer before we had kids. But we were happy when we found out. Why?"

"I'm just wondering how you make that call," I say. "When you know you're ready."

"You thinking about kids?" Caleb asks, his eyebrows drawn together.

"No," I say a little too quickly. "No, it's not... Just something Mia said made me think about the future and making big decisions. That kind of thing. I was just wondering."

"I see. We were young when we got married, and we were both in school, so we figured it made sense to wait. As far as how you make that call, you just talk about it. Melanie and I were really open with each other about everything. We always knew where we stood." He smiles again, but I see the sadness in his eyes. I know he still misses her. "That helped when it came to big decisions."

Damn it, I'm thinking about a future with Mia and I'm already failing at the *being really open with each other* part. I take a sip of my beer. "Remember when we were kids and we used to do that *on a scale of one to ten, how bad would it be* thing?"

"Yeah," he says. "Like, on a scale of one to ten, how bad would it be if we set off fireworks in the dumpster at school?"

"Exactly. Wait, we did that, didn't we?"

He laughs. "Yeah, we did."

"How did we make it to adulthood without getting arrested? Anyway, I've got one for you. On a scale of one to ten, how bad would it be if a guy was friends with a woman online under an anonymous identity, met her in person, started dating her, found out she's his online friend, but didn't tell her who he is?"

"That's *extremely* specific," Caleb says. "I'm guessing this isn't hypothetical."

"Just answer the question."

"Okay, scale of one to ten... I guess that's somewhere around a five, depending on the details. So he—I'll say he, because I guess we're pretending this isn't you—he's friends with her online, but they don't know personal details? Kind of like, what was that Tom Hanks movie? The one with Meg Ryan?"

"*You've Got Mail.*"

"Right. Can we both just admit we've seen it?" I nod and he continues. "So is it like that? Are they rivals but exchanging witty banter over email?"

"No," I say. "They're not rivals, although I guess you could say he knows her professionally."

"Did he know who she was when they started dating?" he asks.

"No, but he figured it out pretty quickly," I say. "She tells her online friend... well, everything."

Caleb blows out a breath. "Shit. So she's telling her friend things about the guy she's dating... and the guy she's dating is her friend? But she doesn't realize it?"

"Yes."

"Okay, we're heading for more like a six or seven at this point," he says. "Why didn't he tell her they know each other once he figured it out?"

I take a deep breath. "At first, because he thought it might threaten his career. And he didn't want to risk it if the relationship wasn't going anywhere."

"But the relationship *is* going somewhere?" Caleb asks.

"I'm in love with her," I say, my voice quiet. "But at this point, I don't know how to tell her who I am."

"Shit, bro," he says.

We sit in silence for a few minutes. I run my thumb up and down the cool glass bottle, tracing a line through the moisture.

"Obviously you have to tell her," Caleb says.

"I know. It's just... complicated. I'm behind on a project at work. Dad's bills are fucking crazy. She's got some stressful family stuff going on. I need to tell her, but I feel like I'm risking everything if I do. I don't know if I can deal with the very real possibility of losing her right now. And yes, I realize how selfish that is."

"Alex, you've been dealing with the burden of everything going on with Dad on your own for, how long now?" he asks.

"It's been a few years," I say. "But I'm not totally on my own. Kendra's around, and you've just been busy with your own shit."

"Sure, but I know you. You've been shouldering this yourself. That's how you are. So right now you're under a shit ton of pressure. I'm not saying it's a good thing you're lying to your girlfriend. You definitely need to tell her. But I don't think you're selfish for wanting to make sure the time is right."

"I don't know what she's going to say when I do. We haven't been together that long, but I'm crazy about her, Caleb. And this could be the thing that does it. The thing that ruins it. It fucking sucks."

"It won't necessarily ruin it," he says. "Especially if you tell her before she finds out on her own."

"Yeah, that's true," I say.

"Trust her," he says. "If she's in love with you too, she'll want to work through it, even if she's mad you didn't tell her."

I take a drink. "I hope you're right."

"So, despite the whole 'she doesn't know you're her online friend' thing, this is cool," he says. "I like seeing you happy."

"Thanks. It's... unexpected."

Caleb smiles. "Sometimes the best things are."

I hang out with my brother for a while. It's nice having him around. We gave each other a lot of shit when we were younger, but as adults, we get along pretty well.

We finish our beers, then sit and chat with Dad. He's not much of a talker, but I can tell he's getting anxious about his surgery. He makes too many jokes about it.

I check the time on my phone. It's not too late, but I'm ready to head home.

"I'll see you guys later," I say.

"Night, Alex," Dad says. He pauses, still looking at me. "Be good to her. I like this one."

"Yeah, Dad. I will."

I say goodnight and head out, my mind filled with thoughts of Mia. Of how I'm going to bring this up. Is there a way I can tell her that isn't going to get me in trouble?

When I get home, I send her a text. I want to make sure we have time to talk soon. Alone.

Me: Hey baby. Today was fun.

It takes a few minutes for her to reply.

Mia: Hi! It was. Sorry. Sleepy.

Me: Sorry, did I wake you?

Mia: It's okay. I love getting your texts. They make me all warm and fuzzy inside.

Me: I won't keep you up. Just thought I'd see if we can get together Saturday.

Mia: Yeah, Shelby will be home by then. Have something in mind?

Me: I'm thinking we stay in. Cozy blankets. Movie. Wine.

Mia: OMG, stop.

Me: Stop what?

Mia: Being so perfect.

Me: Um, not perfect.

Mia: Are you kidding? Let's stay in and snuggle in cozy blankets, drink wine, and watch a movie? That's my favorite ever. You're too perfect.

Me: Definitely not perfect. Trust me.

Mia: I remain unconvinced. We're on for Saturday. But I'm literally falling sleep. My crazy niece will be up before dawn even thinks about cracking.

Me: Get some sleep. Love you, baby.

Mia: Love you too.

24

MIA

I've been looking forward to my stay-in date with Alex all day. I slept another night at Shelby's house, which meant another early summons from Miss Alanna. But Shelby and Daniel got home with baby Danny (that kid is getting a nickname whether Shelby likes it or not) around lunch, so I had time to go home and catch a nap.

Fabio was uncharacteristically clingy. My neighbor Jim had been by twice a day to feed him, but apparently Fabio's cold feline heart does need affection once in a while. Dare I say he missed me? He snuggled up in bed with me while I napped and seemed sad that I was leaving again. Poor kitty.

I glance down at my clothes as I walk up to Alex's apartment. Maybe I took this comfy cozy evening a little too seriously. I'm dressed in a pair of black leggings and a loose blue sweater, with big, thick socks. My slip-on shoes make no sense with socks, but they're easy to get on and off. I figure I'll ditch my shoes at the door anyway, and we aren't going out. I hit the up button on the elevator. Alex never comments on my clothes. I don't think he'll mind, and it's not like I came over wearing flannel pajama pants. I wouldn't go that far.

Okay, so I *almost* came over in pajama pants. Pink ones with ice cream cones all over them. But I didn't. I have some dignity.

Alex smiles at me when he answers the door. "Hey, beautiful. You look cute tonight."

I adjust my glasses and glance down at myself. "Thanks. You said cozy, so..."

"I like you cozy." He brings me in for a kiss, closing the door behind me. "Make yourself comfortable. I'll get some wine and we can pick a movie."

He hesitates for a second, watching me. His brow furrows a little and he takes a deep breath.

"Are you okay?" I ask.

"Yeah," he says. "I'm fine."

I take off my coat and put my purse down while Alex goes into the kitchen. "So, where are these cozy blankets of which you speak?"

"Good question," he says. "Give me a second, and I'll find something."

There's a closet near the door. "Maybe in here?"

I open it and find a few coats, but most of the space is taken up by a stack of boxes. The top one is open, and the contents catch my eye. It's full of books. They look like Lexi Logan books. I pick one up from the top of the stack and flip it open. Not only is it a Lexi Logan book—her latest—it's signed, a big swooping signature with a little heart dotting the *i*.

I know he likes to read, but I didn't think he read these. And why would he have an entire box of the same book? I check another one, and it's signed too. This is so weird.

Alex comes out from the kitchen holding two glasses of wine and stops, his eyes wide.

"Sorry, I was just looking for blankets and I noticed these," I say, holding up the book. "But why do you have an entire box of them? Or, five boxes of them?"

He stares at me with his mouth partially open and the look on his face is only heightening my confusion. Why does he look so guilty?

"Okay." He puts the wine down on the dining table. "This is actually why I invited you over tonight. I need to tell you the truth."

My body tenses up and I swallow hard. His tone is worrying me, like he's about to tell me something awful.

"What truth?" I ask, trying to keep my voice light. "That you secretly love reading romance novels?"

"No," he says. "Actually, I write them."

"What?" I glance at the book in my hand, then back at Alex. "Is this a joke? I don't get it."

He takes a deep breath. "No, it's not a joke. Mia, I'm Lexi Logan. It's the pen name I use. I wrote those books."

It takes a second for what he's saying to sink in. I look at the book again, focusing on the letters of her name. Or is it *his* name? Alex is Lexi? The Lexi who has become my favorite author? My friend? The person I talk to about everything?

The book falls from my limp fingers and I stare at Alex. "Are you serious? You aren't serious. How? No. You can't be."

"I am," he says. "I'm so sorry. I've been planning on telling you. I wanted to tell you. It just never seemed like the right time, and when it did seem right, things kept happening."

My brain tries to recall every conversation I've ever had with Lexi. The times I confided in her. The times I vented to her about a crappy date. All the things I told her about Alex. I thought I was telling an online girlfriend, but I was really talking to *him. About him.* He read everything I said about him.

"Oh my god," I say, stepping away from him. "*Oh my god.* I've been... and you were... this whole time... and it was... Lexi was you?"

"Yes, Lexi was me."

"Holy shit." My stomach turns. "I've been telling you things —things about you. And you've been using that, haven't you? You've been manipulating me this whole time."

"No," he says, putting up a hand. "No, Mia, I swear it wasn't like that."

"How can you say that?" I ask. "Oh my god, it started in the bookstore. *Can I buy you books*? I told Lexi I wished a guy would do that, and you used it on me. You picked me up with my own line."

"No. God, Mia, I didn't know who you were then," he says. "I just thought you were cute and it seemed like a good idea."

"When did you know?" I ask.

His brow furrows, but he doesn't answer.

"Alex, when did you find out who I was?"

"After we had dinner at Lift," he says. "You messaged Lexi and talked about your date. I knew it had to be me."

I gape at him. That was our *first* dinner date. He's known that long? "How could you keep this from me?"

"The only person who knows about this is my sister," he says. "I keep it from everybody else."

"Yeah? Well you aren't sleeping with everybody else," I say.

He winces. "Mia, please. I didn't mean to lie to you."

"Of course you meant to," I say. "It's not like lying happens by accident."

"No, but I wanted to tell you," he says. "I swear, I was going to."

I meet his eyes and cross my arms. "But you didn't. Why?"

He takes a deep breath. "Mia, you run one of the biggest book blogs in the genre. What if things didn't work out between us, and you decided to out me?"

"That's what you think of me? That I'd become some disgruntled ex-girlfriend and blast your real identity all over the Internet?"

"No, I don't think that now," he says. "But when we first met, I simply didn't know. I didn't know you."

"Yes, you did," I say. Tears burn my eyes, but I do *not* want to cry in front of him. "You knew me in a way most people don't. I thought Lexi and I were good friends. I was really open with her. Once you figured out who I was, you should have realized you knew me very well."

"Okay, so we were friends for a long time," he says. "I get it. But it's not like we both weren't anonymous. You were too."

I gape at him, so angry I can barely speak. "Hold on there. I'm not the one who's been lying. If I'd figured out who you were, I would have told you. And I did tell you I had a blog. I told you everything, and you still lied to me."

"I was going to tell you, right then," he says. "But your sister called."

"She was having a baby!"

"I know, but her timing was fucking awful."

"As if she had any control over that," I say. "This isn't Shelby's fault, you asshole. It's yours. And then you *still* didn't tell me."

"That was just the other day," he says. "I've barely seen you since then. It's not like I was going to tell you I write romance novels while we were having fake tea with our nieces."

"This isn't about you writing romance novels," I say. "This is about you lying to me. I thought you were someone else. I thought Lexi was someone else. God, I feel like such an idiot."

I turn away, my mind reeling. All this time, I kept thinking he was too perfect. This couldn't be real.

I guess I was right.

"Mia..."

"This is why you seemed so perfect," I say. "You've studied all this shit, haven't you? So you can write it. You knew exactly what to do, every step of the way. No wonder I felt like I was living in a fucking romance novel."

"No," he says. "That's not... I didn't... God, Mia, nothing I said or did was fake or planned. I wasn't trying to pull something on you. We met and it was like being hit by a meteor. Everything has been happening so fast."

"Too fast, obviously," I say.

"Look, I know I should have told you," he says. "I've been agonizing over how to explain everything."

"Less agonizing and more telling would have been a good start. Maybe around the time you realized who I was. But you let me go on believing Lexi was someone else, even when I was sharing things about you. About us." I grab my coat and purse and head for the door. I can't stay here. This is all too much and I need to get away so I can process what just happened. My stomach feels like it dropped to the floor and my heart is beating too fast. A sob tries to escape my throat, but I force it back down. "I don't know who you are anymore. I have to go."

"Mia, please—"

I'm out the door before I hear the rest.

25

MIA

*E*motional whiplash is fucking brutal.

Fabio curls up next to me on the couch. I scratch behind his ears while I blow on my mug of tea. Somehow I've managed to get through the last few days—even dealing with work. But it hasn't been easy. My mind is a disaster, and don't even get me started on the space where my heart used to be. It's so hollow, like an empty warehouse with a soaring ceiling and concrete walls that make every sound echo.

Alex finally stopped texting today. I haven't read a single one. It's not that I'm such a bitch that I'll never read what he has to say. I just can't yet. Finding out he's Lexi caught me completely by surprise, and it's taking me a while to sort through everything.

The thing is, I didn't just fall for Alex. I crashed for him. It's classic Mia, when you think about it. Normal girls would have held a little of their heart back—kept themselves in check. Me? I tripped, stumbled, fell, and made it awkward. I swooned so hard I basically stopped thinking. How could I not have realized who he was?

Okay, that's a little harsh. Who would have imagined that the man I was dating was the romance author I'd come to consider one of my best friends? That's not really something you watch out for. Normally you're on the lookout for signs that a guy is married, or unemployed, or a criminal or something. But female alter ego who is the friend you always confide in? Yeah, not something I could have predicted.

But I should have known something was off. He never talked about his job, at least not with any specifics. He just said he was a consultant, and he worked from home. I think the most detail I ever got was when he told me he was "behind on a project." It didn't occur to me to wonder what that project was. What a "consultant" actually did. I never asked. I just took him at his word and didn't think about it.

There were other signs that I missed. He slipped once and referred to *special panties*—a phrase I'd used with Lexi. He often seemed to know things, or act unsurprised when I shared something. Of course, they were things he already knew, because I'd told Lexi.

And the way Lexi reacted when I talked about Alex... Short replies. Always making an excuse about having to go. It bothered me, but I could never pinpoint the reason.

I guess now I know.

I feel so stupid. It's embarrassing to think about all the things I told Lexi about Alex. He was on the other end of all those conversations. I told her how great our dates were. How I felt about him. What did I call the sex? Book-worthy? I suppose he didn't mind hearing that. I told him my ovaries were exploding, for fuck's sake. I talked to Lexi like I would a close girlfriend. I'm sure I shared any number of mortifying things since we became friends.

And he knew. He knew who I was, almost from the beginning. How could he not tell me?

His explanation that he was afraid I'd out him on my blog is so insulting. He really thought I would be that petty? It wasn't like I was some random girl he just met. Once he figured out who I was, he should have known he could trust me.

I take a sip of my tea and it burns my tongue. "Shit."

Fabio cracks an eye open. He's been unusually affectionate since I got home from work today. I didn't think cats could ping off the emotions of their owners the way dogs do, but Fabio has my back tonight. His soft fur and rhythmic purring are keeping me from completely losing it.

I glance at my laptop. One of the worst parts about all of this is that the person I'd normally go to when I'm upset or nursing a broken heart is Lexi. Obviously that's no longer an option.

I didn't just lose my boyfriend. I lost a good friend too. Maybe my best friend. Lexi was the first person I talked to whenever I had something to share—good or bad. I'm not great at making friends, and my propensity for staying home and reading means my social life is a little bit lackluster. But Lexi was always there for me. She commiserated with me when I had bad dates, gave me pep talks when I was down on myself. She made me laugh on my worst days.

My heart aches with the pain of everything I've lost. And I feel like I don't have anyone to talk to. I can't even make myself get lost in a book. Lexi books always had this way of bringing everything full circle. She'd break my heart, but always stitch it back together with just the right words.

I don't think Alex has the words to fix this.

With a deep breath, I bring up Shelby's number. She's busy with her new baby, but maybe she'll have time to talk. I have all these emotions swirling around inside. I need to get them out or I'm going to go fucking crazy.

"Hey Mia," she says when she answers. "What's up?"

"Are you busy?" I ask. "If you're busy, it's fine. I know your life is so crazy right now."

"I'm okay, actually," she says. "Baby Daniel slept for five hours last night, and I got in a nap today. I actually feel human."

"That's awesome."

"You okay?" she asks. "You sound weird."

"Not really." I pause, trying to gather the courage I need to tell my sister what's going on. At this point, I might as well tell her everything. "It's a bit of a long story, but it begins with: Alex and I kind of broke up."

"Oh, Mia," she says.

To my surprise, Shelby listens quietly while I tell her everything. I tell her about being Bookworm Babe, and how big my blog is. How I struck up a friendship with Lexi Logan, my favorite romance author. How it turns out that Lexi is Alex, and he didn't tell me who he was. She doesn't lecture me about my reading habits, or comment on the fact that I spend a lot of time running a blog. She doesn't ask what I did to screw things up with Alex. In fact, she doesn't comment much, other than interjecting a few words here and there so I know she's listening.

"Wow," she says after I finish. "I'm not even sure what to say. So you haven't talked to him since you found out?"

"No," I say. "He's texted me a bunch of times, but I haven't read them. I don't think I can deal with it yet."

"Don't do that thing you do, Mia," she says.

"What thing?"

"The thing where you go inward," she says. "I can hear it in your voice. You're ready to retreat into your own little world. You've been going to work, right?"

"Yeah," I say. "I'm not going to lose my job over this."

"Good," she says. "I'm glad you finally called. I don't want you isolating yourself."

"Shelby, I'm not."

"You should come up this weekend," she says.

"Okay, calm down," I say. "I'm not isolating."

"I'm serious," she says. "And you should read his texts. What he did was shitty, but maybe you should at least talk to him."

"I guess, but I feel like I can't trust anything he says."

"Do you think he was lying to you about everything?" she asks. "Or just his pen name?"

"It isn't just that he has a pen name," I say. "He and I were talking online all the time and he didn't tell me who he was."

"I understand," Shelby says. "I'm just wondering if you think everything else was bullshit."

"That's the problem, I don't know. I don't know what to believe. For all I know, he was just playing me the whole time."

"I'm sorry, Mia," Shelby says.

I wait for a second, expecting her to qualify that somehow. But she doesn't say anything else.

"Thanks, Shelby."

"Listen, don't be worried that you're intruding on us. Daniel is off work for the next three weeks and Alanna is adjusting really well. If you need to come up and eat junk food and bitch about men, I'm here. I can barely do anything after two surgeries, so I wouldn't mind the company."

I laugh. "Bitching about men with you isn't very fun. You don't have anything to bitch about."

"Honey, you have no idea," she says. "But still, come up this weekend. Don't shut out the world, okay?"

"I won't."

"I need to go feed the baby, but I'll talk to you later."

"Give him squishy kisses from his auntie," I say.

"I will."

I hit end and look at my phone—at the little six by my text messaging app, showing my unread messages. At the messenger app I always used to chat with Lexi. They stare at me, daring me to open them.

I toss my phone on the other end of the couch. The thought

of looking at something he wrote makes my stomach turn over and a fresh wave of tears threaten to fall. I've cried myself sense-less every night since I left him. I keep thinking I'll eventually cry myself out. But the tightness in my chest returns and I feel the telltale lump rising in my throat. Anguish washes over me, hitting me like an ocean wave.

Why does this have to hurt so much?

I get up, stumble into my bedroom, and fall onto the bed. I'm still dressed, but I don't care. Fabio follows me in. He jumps up and stretches, rounding his back. He blinks at me a few times, then curls up, his soft purrs vibrating against me as we both fall asleep.

26

ALEX

*C*hecking my phone again isn't going to make a message from Mia magically appear, but I do it anyway. Still nothing. I keep trying to text her, but if she's reading them, she's not responding.

It's been days. I'd call, but I know she won't answer. I tell myself she just needs time. She can't shut me out forever.

But each day her silence scares me a little more.

It's not like I didn't see this coming. I knew this could blow up in my face. Even if she hadn't opened that closet and found the books, I was going to tell her. That night probably would have ended the same way, even if we'd been on the couch and I'd simply said, "Mia, I have something to tell you."

Either way, losing her is fucking devastating.

I miss her like she was oxygen and now I'm left to suffocate. My lungs burn with every breath. I've been going through the motions of each day, but my heart isn't in anything. Emails pile up. Social media messages go unanswered. Just the thought of writing is a joke. I can't write about people falling in love when I've ruined the best thing I ever had.

I don't know if I'll ever write again.

The reality of what that means is not lost on me. My dad is having surgery tomorrow and the medical bills aren't going anywhere. I need to keep the Lexi train going if I'm going to get him through this. But that's a lot easier said than done when all I can do is sit in front of my laptop and stare.

I need to find a way to make Mia understand how much she means to me. How I'll do anything to regain her trust. That I'll wait as long as it takes, even though it's killing me.

I need to fight for her, but I'm not sure what to do. She won't talk to me. If I thought there was any chance she'd let me in, I'd go over to her place right now. Even though that's exactly what I want to do, I know it would be wrong. I know she needs space.

I just really fucking hate it.

My phone dings with a text and my heart feels like it stopped. I pick it up quickly, hoping it's Mia. My shoulders slump and I breathe out a long breath. It's my sister.

Kendra: You coming tonight?

Me: Coming where?

Kendra: Dinner at Dad's. He goes in for surgery tomorrow.

Fuck. The last thing I want to do is go have dinner with my family. But I can't ignore my dad right now.

Me: Yeah, I'll be over in a bit. Can I bring anything?

Kendra: No, we have it covered.

A couple hours later—and still no message from Mia—I head to my dad's house. I resolve to act as normal as possible so they won't ask me any awkward questions. That lasts all of two minutes until Kendra asks about Mia. I try to brush off her question with a noncommittal answer, but I know she can see through me.

I get through dinner, and everyone keeps the conversation light. None of us want to stress out Dad. He seems fine, although I notice when he retires to his recliner with his nightly drink, his glass is fuller than usual. Caleb gets Charlotte off to bed while Kendra and I clean up the kitchen.

Caleb comes back as Kendra puts the last of the dishes away. He glances at her, then leans in and lowers his voice. "So, did you talk to Mia yet?"

"Yeah. It was about as shitty as you could imagine."

"Damn," he says. "Is that it? You guys broke up over it?"

I shrug. "I guess. She left and she hasn't spoken to me since."

"Who hasn't spoken to you?" Kendra asks.

"God, nosy woman," I say.

"Are you talking about Mia?" she asks.

I blow out a breath. "Yeah."

"What happened?" She waves us both over to the kitchen table, so Caleb and I join her.

This is ridiculous. Each of them knows part of the story, but neither of them knows everything. And now I have to tell my younger brother that I write romance novels. Fucking hell.

"Okay, I need to back up. Caleb, I'm not a consultant. I've been making my living as a writer."

"That's great," he says. "Is that a secret or something? Why didn't you tell us?"

"Because I write romance novels."

Caleb raises his eyebrows at me. "Come again?"

"I write romance novels," I say. "I know, that sounds crazy. But apparently I'm pretty good at it."

"He's amazing," Kendra says. "His books are very good and his readers love them."

"You knew about this?" Caleb asks.

"Yeah, I've been helping," Kendra says.

"She's literally the only one in the world who knew," I say. "I write under a female pen name, and I haven't told anybody."

"I'm glad you're willing to own this," Kendra says. "But what does this have to do with Mia?"

I take another deep breath. "Mia has an online identity too. She's a book blogger. I actually met her online well before she and I met in person. We became really good friends, although she thought I was a woman. When we did meet in person, I had no idea who she was. But I figured out it, and I kind of didn't tell her."

"Everything makes so much sense now," Caleb says.

"For fuck's sake, Alex," Kendra says.

"Yeah, I know. I don't need you to tell me what a dumbass I am. I'm well aware."

"How did she find out?" Kendra asks.

"I was going to tell her," I say. "I literally invited her over on Saturday so we could talk. But she found my boxes of Lexi books for the giveaway before I had a chance to say anything. Not that it would have made much of a difference. The damage had already been done. I've been lying to her almost since the beginning."

"Wow," Kendra says. "I guess that means she didn't take it well."

"No, she didn't," I say.

"This sucks," Kendra says. "What are you going to do?"

"I don't know. I've texted her, but she isn't responding."

"Maybe she just needs some time," Caleb says. "I bet you'll hear from her soon."

"Fuck, I hope so. I think she needs space, but it's hard to give it to her. I want to go over there and make her listen to me."

"Not a good idea," Kendra says. "Damn it, why didn't I become better friends with her? I could be, like, the liaison between you two."

"I don't think that would help," I say.

"Okay, so if you can't talk to her, what else can you do?" Kendra asks. "Just wait to see if she answers you?"

I shrug. "That's where I'm at."

"I'm sorry, Alex," Kendra says.

"Yeah, this is rough," Caleb says.

"It sucks," I say. "We were so good together. I loved everything about her. The way she got tongue-tied and the funny things she said. Her smile, her eyes. I wasn't looking for someone like her. I wasn't looking for anyone. But suddenly, there she was, and everything changed. Now I'm afraid I ruined it and I won't have the chance to get her back."

"You will," Kendra says.

She sounds sure of herself, but I know she's just trying to make me feel better.

"You should write to her," Caleb says.

"I tried. She's not responding."

"Not a text," he says. "Write her a letter. You're good with words. That's what you do. I know you can't make her read it, but maybe she'll respond to something like that."

I nod, the words already starting to form in my mind. "That's not a bad idea."

"That's why they pay me the big bucks," he says with a smile.

I get up and grab my coat. "That's actually a great idea. I have to go."

I'm out the door before they have a chance to say anything else. Caleb is right. I am good with words, and that's how I can get through to her. But I'm not going to write her a letter. I'm going to write her a story.

Our story.

I just hope I can get her to read it.

27

MIA

*A*lthough I've worked in and around hospitals for several years, I don't think I'll ever get used to the harsh, biting odor that permeates them. I head for the fourth floor, wondering for the millionth time if I should be here, my nose burning from the smell. My office is across the street from the main hospital, and I tried to do this yesterday at lunch. I didn't make it past the parking lot. This time, I'm all the way to the elevator.

I clutch a folder of paperwork to my chest. It's a vague excuse for being here. Ken Lawson is on my patient roster, but I don't have a real reason to go see him while he's in recovery after his surgery. I'll help coordinate his aftercare and physical therapy, but those are things I do on the phone, sitting at my desk. I grabbed his file anyway. The truth is, I want to go see him. Even though I've only met him a few times, he's such a nice man, and I want to make sure he's doing okay.

And fine, I can admit the fact that he's Alex's dad has something to do with it.

I still haven't talked to Alex. I broke down and read his texts a couple days ago. They said everything I expected them to say. *I'm sorry. Can we please talk? I miss you. I love you.*

Yeah, sure you do. Not enough to be honest, apparently.

My boots click on the tiles and butterflies swirl through my tummy as I walk down the hallway. I pause outside room fourten and take a deep breath. Here goes nothing.

The head of Ken's bed is partially raised, so he's at an incline. He's wearing a blue hospital gown and beige blankets cover his legs. His eyebrows lift in surprise when he sees me in the doorway.

"Is that Mia?" he asks.

"Yeah, hi there." I come into the room and stand next to the bed, holding the folder against my body. "I just came to see how you're doing."

His eyes crinkle at the corners with his smile. "Better than expected. They got me up so I could walk around this morning. I took four whole steps."

"That's great," I say. "How's your pain?"

"Oh, it's fine," he says. "I can handle it, and I'd rather have my wits about me. Especially when pretty young ladies come to visit me."

I smile. "Can I get you anything?"

"No, the nurses are taking good care of me," he says.

"Good. Well, I just wanted to see how everything is going since your surgery."

"That's nice of you. Do you have paperwork for me to sign or something?" He gestures to the folder.

"Oh, no, not really." I shift the folder and a few papers slip out the bottom. I crouch down to grab them and tuck them back in. "You're all set for now."

He nods. "All right."

"I should let you rest." I reach out and touch his arm. "I'm glad you're doing well. Everything is arranged for your transfer to the rehab facility. Dr. Lander will have to make the call to release you, but once he does, you're good to go."

He smiles again, a look that reminds me so much of his son. "Thank you, Mia."

"Of course," I say, squeezing his arm.

I turn and crash into a wall, sending papers flying in every direction. Only it isn't a wall. It's a man. A tall, gorgeous man with a shirt that's half untucked, a beard that's thicker than usual, and hair that looks like he just got out of bed.

"Oh shit, I'm sorry," Alex says.

We both crouch down and pick up the papers. He meets my eyes as he hands them to me. My heart nearly beats out of my chest. He looks so unkempt—his hair, his beard, his rumpled clothes. He's so adorable and sad I almost jump into his arms.

But I don't; I hold back. I stand and tuck the last of the papers back in the folder.

Alex rubs the back of his neck. "Hi. Sorry about that. Can I talk to you outside? Please?"

I glance back at Ken and try to smile, but there's too much turmoil raging inside me. I give Alex a brief nod and walk out of the room, stopping a few feet from the door.

"I didn't expect you to be here, but I'm so glad to see you," Alex says.

"I'm not... I mean... I came to..." I take a breath. "I was just checking on your dad."

"Yeah, I heard you talking," he says. "It's really nice of you to come see him. I know you didn't have to."

Damn it, his voice is so disarming. And he looks so messy and sweet. I want to kiss every inch of him. "Are you okay? You look so disheveled."

He glances down at himself. "Oh, yeah. I've been... I've been busy with something. I guess I haven't been sleeping much this last week."

A crack snakes across the wall I'm trying to keep between us.

No, Mia. He lied about everything. You can't trust him.

"So, maybe we could go get some coffee?" he asks. "Or lunch?"

"I really can't," I say. "I have to get back to work."

"Right." He puts his hands in his pockets. "Sorry, I don't mean to keep you."

The forlorn tone in his voice pisses me off. He's the one who lied to me. Why does he get to be sad? I should look like a mess, not him. But here I am, dressed in work clothes, handling my shit. My hair is brushed. He couldn't be bothered to at least run his fingers through his? He doesn't get to be the sad victim in this breakup. It's *his* fault.

I straighten my shoulders and make sure my grip on the paperwork is firm so I don't drop the folder again. "Your dad's transfer to the rehab center is all arranged. Dr. Lander just needs to approve the move based on his progress here."

Alex blinks at me. "Yeah. Of course. Thank you."

"It's fine. It's my job. Which I have to go back to." I turn and swallow hard, my eyes stinging. I will not cry. I will not let these traitorous tears betray me in front of him.

"Mia."

I stop, but keep my back to him. I wait for the space of three heartbeats, but Alex doesn't say anything else. Without looking back, I walk away.

I'm an absolute wreck by the time I get back to my desk. My boss is out of the office, so I send him a quick email, claiming to be sick. I've tried so hard not to let my personal life get in the way of my job, but after seeing Alex, I'm just done.

I get home, strip out of my work clothes, put on my pink pajama pants and an old t-shirt, and collapse on the couch. Fabio meows at me a few times before I realize he thinks it's time for me to feed him. I'm home early, and he really doesn't need to eat, but I get up and pour food into his dish anyway. I'd rather just give him what he wants than deal with him bothering me for the next couple hours.

Seeing Alex sent me right back to square one. Not that I was anywhere near getting over him. But it was like ripping open a wound that was only just starting to heal.

It *hurts*.

I'm angry that such a quick encounter with him could do this to me. I ran home to hide after one chance meeting with him. I grab my green blanket and pull it around my shoulders. Fucking feelings. Although I suppose being hurt and angry is better than the awful hollowness I was living with before. At least now I can feel *something* again.

As much as I don't want to be curious about what he's doing, I wonder what he's been working on that has him losing sleep. Probably another stupid Lexi book. Goodness knows he can't let that money-maker lose momentum. What a bunch of shit. He's writing these beautiful love stories and he sucks at making one work in real life.

Fabio jumps up on the couch and meows at me.

"What? I fed you, oh feline master. What more do you want from your human slave?"

He rubs his head against my hand, a clear directive to pet him.

"Fine, here, have some attention."

I scratch his head and pet down his back. He tolerates me for a minute or two, then flops onto his side and bats at my hand.

"Watch it, dickhead. No claws."

His eyes drift closed. Cats are so lazy. But I think he has the right idea; a nap does sound good. I lie down with my legs near Fabio, giving him space so he doesn't decide to attack me in my sleep, and close my eyes.

My phone wakes me up. I blink a few times, trying to force

my brain to start working again. Sometimes naps leave you feeling refreshed. Other times you sleep so hard, you barely know where you are when you open your eyes.

I'm struggling with the latter.

"What's up?" I ask Fabio, although he's still sleeping. I reach over and grab my phone. I have a text. Great, now I have to decide if I should look. If it's from Alex, I don't think I'll be able to resist reading it. But it might be from work, or from Shelby. If it's from my boss, I need to answer it. I did bail out of work early. And if it's from Shelby, she'll get all weird if I don't answer right away. She's been bugging me on a daily basis to make sure I don't "go hermit."

Okay, Mia. Deep breath.

I swipe my thumb across the screen. The text is from Alex. And I was right; I can't resist reading it.

Turn on your Kindle.

What the hell? My Kindle is on the coffee table. I don't even know if it's charged. I haven't read a book since things blew up with Alex. I know as soon as I turn it on, I'll be faced with a host of Lexi Logan covers. I just can't deal with that.

Should I do it? Should I look? I'm torn between wanting to angrily delete his text and ignore his request, and a burning curiosity as to what I'll find if I do turn it on.

I stare at my Kindle for a long moment before curiosity wins.

I power it on. There's not a lot of battery left, but I tell myself I don't need much. I'm just going to look and then promptly ignore whatever he sent. He wouldn't be such an asshole as to send me an advance copy of his next Lexi book, would he?

Something starts downloading. I wait, my heart rate rising as it loads. A cover appears. It has a man with a woman facing him, almost in his lap. His hands are on her waist, and her long brown hair obscures some of her face. Their mouths are together in a kiss. It's beautiful—the sort of cover I once told

Lexi I wish I saw more often. At the bottom are the title and author name:

Book Boyfriend
Alex Lawson

I tap on it to open the book. The words on the first page hit me like a punch to the gut.

For Mia.

What the fuck is this? He dedicates a book to me and he thinks that's going to make things better? My breath coming fast, I swipe again.

Chapter One
Alex

Wait, what? This is... Oh my god. I navigate to the table of contents. The chapters are all named either *Alex* or *Mia*. Holy shit, did he write a book about *us*?

I hit the power button and toss my Kindle back on the table. Fuck this. I'm not reading this. Burning curiosity or no, I'm not reading it. Ever.

I'll just have to get a new Kindle and start a new account. I'm never turning that one on again.

MY RESOLVE LASTS two entire days. I don't turn on my Kindle. Fine, I do plug it in so it's charged, but that's just being practical. I'm going through some serious book withdrawal, so I'll just

read other things. I'll staunchly ignore Alex's book and find
something else.

Maybe.

All right, that's a crock of shit. I'm not fooling anyone.

I sit down on the couch with the Device of Evil Temptation
and snuggle up in my favorite blanket. Fabio glances up at me
from his spot on his kitty bed across the room.

"Don't judge me, asshole cat. How long was I supposed to
last? I've been a fucking brick wall for two days. We both knew
I'd crack eventually."

Fabio goes back to sleep, like he's bored of my drama.

I turn it on, open the book, take a deep breath, and start
reading.

IT's everything I hoped and everything I feared it would be. It
starts with me finding the Lexi Logan books in Alex's closet, as if
that was the pivotal moment in our story. It goes back to explain
how Alex became Lexi Logan. I read about Lexi and BB's friendship. Running into Alex (literally) in the bookstore. How he
found out who I was, and decided to stay away. Seeing each
other at his dad's appointment and his decision to ask me out
again. Our dates. My power going out. The sex—oh god, he can
write sex, but the real thing was still better. Meeting his family.
The tea party with our nieces. All our moments are there, everything that led us to that awful night when he told me he's Lexi.

And somehow, he makes more sense. I didn't think about the
pressures of caring for his dad, or what his earnings as Lexi
meant to his family. I should have. I was there when he told his
dad he'd pay for his surgery. That was no small chunk of change.
That's why he was so worried about telling me in the beginning.
Granted, he shouldn't have balked. He should have known me as

BB well enough to trust me with his secret. But as much as I hate to admit it, I can understand why he didn't. He has a lot riding on being Lexi.

His portrayal of me is nothing short of uncanny. He took some liberties with what I was thinking, as he'd have to. It's not like he's *actually* in my head. But he's so close, it's kind of scary.

If this story is anything close to accurate—and there's no way I can deny that it is—he did want to tell me. We were both caught up in something that took us by surprise. Neither of us expected to fall in love so fast. It was all so crazy.

Damn it, I think he was trying to do the right thing.

The last chapter describes Alex having a conversation with his brother and sister. Caleb tells him to do what he does best— use his words. Alex rushes home and, in a fury of creative passion, with lots of coffee and very little sleep, he writes. He writes our story, pouring his heart out onto the page. With dry, gritty eyes, messy hair, and a full beard, he finally finishes. His heart sits in his throat as he sends it to my Kindle, all his hope resting on his words.

I turn the page, tears burning my eyes.

THIS STORY DOESN'T HAVE *an end. Not yet. If it were truly a work of fiction, I know exactly what I would write. Mia would read this book and it would open her heart to me. She'd realize how much I love her. That I would do anything to regain her trust. And she'd come back to me, running into my waiting arms. I would embrace her, feel her soft skin, breathe in the scent of her hair.*

If I could write this ending, I would finish it with the ultimate happily ever after.

28

ALEX

$\mathcal{T}$wo days.

It's been two days since I sent Mia the book. I had her send-to-Kindle address from giving her advance copies of Lexi books, so I know she got it. Whether she opened it, let alone read it, is another story. She hasn't answered my text. I haven't heard a word.

Two days.

I've showered, changed clothes, trimmed my beard. I ran errands, answered emails, caught up on social media. I knocked out an outline for a new Lexi book. I visited my dad and helped him get settled in the rehab center. I've done everything I can to keep my mind off Mia and whether or not she's reading the book I wrote for her.

But nights are the worst. I'm sitting on my couch, alone, with nothing but silence and a glass of Jameson to keep me company.

I want to believe I'll hear from her. I don't have a Plan B. If she doesn't respond, I don't know what to do next. I poured everything I have into that book. Every last bit of hope I have for us. It's all there, in my words. If that isn't enough, nothing will be.

If that isn't enough, I've really lost her.

My phone lights up. It's someone trying to contact me on Lexi's messenger account. I open it and see the name: Bookworm Babe.

Oh, shit. I'm hit with a pang of anxiety as I open the message.

BB: Hi.

Me: Hey.

BB: So, we haven't talked in a while. Looks like you've been busy.

Me: Yeah. I got pretty wrapped up in some personal stuff.

BB: Me too. Personal stuff is hard.

Me: It really is.

BB: This crazy thing happened to me. Wanna hear about it?

Me: Yeah, of course.

BB: Okay, so I met this guy. Alex. You know him.

Me: Sure do.

BB: Well, I fell for this guy. Hard. Not normal person hard. Mia hard. Which means I fell flat on my face in the most embarrassing way possible.

Me: Is that what you think? Because you're really not the embarrassing one in this story.

BB: Maybe not, but hear me out. Our romance was right out of a book. Gorgeous, swoon-worthy hero. Heroine who feels out of her league. Lots of big feels. Crazy hot sex. He swept me off my feet and even managed to catch me when I tripped—most of the time. We were ridiculously compatible and everything kept escalating, as if nothing bad could ever happen. Until...

Me: Until?

BB: Until, just like in a book, we hit a crisis.

Me: We sure did.

BB: He wasn't telling me the whole truth about who he was. And that hurt. I felt betrayed. Like he didn't trust me.

Me: Mia

BB: Wait. Stop typing.

Me: Okay.

There's a long pause while the little dots move. I rub my chin and resist the urge to get up and pace while she types. Finally, her message appears.

BB: I read the book. It's beautiful. I was mad at first, and I didn't want to read it, especially when I realized what it was. But I couldn't stop myself. I finished earlier and took some time to think. And now I'm messaging you because this way I won't get tongue tied.

First of all, I'm sorry I've been ignoring you. I was angry and hurt and not sure how to process what I was feeling. I needed some time.

I've been questioning everything. Lexi. Alex. Who you really are, and what parts were true. As I read the book, a lot of things made more sense. I don't like that you didn't tell me you were Lexi right away. I'm kind of embarrassed that I told you things about you, thinking you weren't you.

But then I realized, none of that scared you away.

I'm this weird, awkward mess of a girl. But you actually like all those parts of me. You catch things when I drop them. You keep me from falling on my face. You don't laugh at me when I blurt things out that I don't mean to say. You don't tease me for the things I love.

I kept saying you were perfect, and I was wrong. You're not perfect. But neither am I. We're both human. We're imperfect and messy and sometimes we make mistakes.

But we're perfect for each other.

That was the point of the book, wasn't it? To show me what you already saw. That we fit together perfectly.

I wait to see if she's going to keep typing but she doesn't. I'm not sure if she's done, or if she's going to say more. Just as I start to reply, there's a knock at my door.

I get up to answer it, adrenaline pumping through my system. God, I hope it's her. Please let it be Mia.

I open the door.

"Hi," Mia says. Her hair is loose around her face, and she's dressed in jeans and a t-shirt with a blue plaid flannel over the top. She pushes her dark-rimmed glasses up her nose.

Fucking hell, I missed her so much.

"Come here." I grab her and pull her into my apartment. I wrap her in my arms and hold her close, breathing in her scent. It floods through me like a drug, lighting up my brain, surging through my body.

She rests her head against my chest and holds me, her arms around my waist, her hands splayed across my back. I take deep breaths, savoring her. She sniffs, and I think maybe she's crying, so I squeeze her tighter.

Relief overwhelms me and I take a few deep breaths to make sure I keep my shit together.

I kiss the top of her head. "God, I missed you."

Her voice is muffled against my shirt. "I missed you too."

I pull back and touch her face. "I really do love you. I swear I never lied about that."

"I know. I love you too. So much." She wipes the tears from beneath her eyes. "Thank you for the book. It's... it's everything."

"I'm glad you liked it."

"I loved it."

I smile at her. "It's only for you."

"I can't... I was... I mean..." She takes a breath and closes her eyes for a second. "I don't remember what else I was going to say. I'm having trouble thinking right now because you smell so good."

"Baby, you don't need to say anything else. Just let me kiss you."

"Yes, please."

I cup her cheeks in my hands and press my mouth to hers. I kiss her softly, relishing the feel of her lips, breathing in her intoxicating scent. She tilts her face, parting her lips, and I deepen the kiss. Her arms wrap around my neck and I pull her to me, holding her close.

Her hand slides down to my cock and she rubs me through my pants. I groan into her mouth and start backing up toward my bedroom.

Leaving a trail of clothes behind us, we make it to my bed. I lie her down and take her mouth in a hard kiss. I pause long enough to get a condom, and then climb back on top of her.

When I slide my cock inside her, everything feels right again. I kiss her everywhere—her forehead, her face, her neck. I want to devour every inch of her.

"Baby, I love you so much," I say softly into her ear.

She runs her hands down my back. "I love you too."

I make love to her, slowly, tenderly. Neither of us can get enough. She begs me for more, and I fuck her harder. Deeper. Give her everything she wants. Everything she needs. I love every bit of her, pouring everything I feel for her into this moment.

We come together in a climax that knocks the breath from my lungs. My body goes rigid, my vision blurs. I'm overwhelmed with the surge of passion, the feel of her coming underneath me.

I stay on top of her for long moments after we finish. She clings to me, her arms around my neck, as if she needs to pull me closer. I kiss her again, deep and slow. Caress her mouth with mine.

"I love you, baby."

"I love you, too."

I keep her in my arms and hold her close. I'll never let her go again.

～

FOR A GUY who writes romance novels for a living, I sure did screw up the love story in my own life. But as you can see, even a man like me can find his happily ever after.

"But wait," you might be saying. "Sure, Mia came back to you. But that's not *quite* a happily ever after, now is it? Come on, man, don't leave us hanging!"

You know what, you have a point. I do still have an epilogue to write.

EPILOGUE

MIA

*F*abio looks up at me through half open eyes. He's curled up near my feet, doing his *I want to be near you but don't touch me* thing. He really is an asshole cat. But I love him anyway.

I tuck my feet under my blanket. "Go back to sleep, fat cat. You already had dinner."

"He seems like he's adjusting to his new digs pretty well," Alex says.

"I'm just glad he hasn't peed on the floor."

Boxes still take up about half of Alex's living room. Or should I say *our* living room. He asked me to move in with him a few weeks ago. Living together was a no-brainer, but we disagreed on whose apartment to keep—his or mine. I argued that mine has more character. He argued that his has double the square footage and more reliable utilities. I had to give him points on both counts.

Fabio decided it for me. After my building had a power outage *and* a plumbing disaster—both in the same week—someone set off the sprinkler system. My entire apartment was soaked, including Fabio. He looked up at me, wet orange fur plastered to his body, and I'm pretty sure he said, "We're moving."

Alex and I did agree that my couch is ten times more comfortable, so he got rid of his. Now I'm lying on my gray cushions of coziness, my feet covered by my favorite blanket, my Kindle in my hands. The click of Alex typing as he writes his next Lexi novel is the only thing breaking the comfortable silence. I have a hot mug of tea nearby, a new book to read, and sure, a lot of unpacking left to do. But that can wait. It'll be there for me tomorrow.

I'm not sure how my life could be any more perfect.

Alex's Lexi Logan pen name is still going strong. Honestly, I think his books just keep getting better. I stopped reviewing them on my blog—it felt like a conflict of interest—but I do announce when "she" has a new release. My little bit of influence certainly isn't needed. He writes books that his readers love. His work speaks for itself.

I do get to be the first to read them, and we've even started brainstorming ideas together. It's one of our favorite date night pastimes—sitting over coffee or a good meal, pinging ideas back and forth.

And his pen name? It's our little secret.

Well, ours, plus Kendra and Caleb. Kendra was always on Team Lexi, and I think Caleb likes having something to tease his big brother about.

Ken's surgery proved to be a success and he's been walking better than he has in years. I'm pretty sure Alex had tears in his eyes the first time he saw his dad moving around without his walker. Kendra and I both cried like babies.

"Are you enjoying your book?" Alex asks.

I look up. "It's okay. Why?"

"You're smiling," he says.

"Am I?" I am smiling, although I wasn't aware of it. "I guess I'm just in a good mood."

"Me too," he says. "Hey can you read something for me?"

"Of course," I say. "What is it?"

"It's an epilogue."

"Really?" I ask. "I didn't think you were that close to being finished."

"Oh, it's for something else," he says. "It's something I left off a while ago. But I'd like to get it wrapped up now. I *think* I'm ready to show it to you."

"Sure. Send it over."

He types for a second. "Incoming."

I navigate back to the menu on my Kindle and see an untitled document load. I open it and start reading.

THE STACK of boxes sits in the corner, a gentle reminder of change, and of work still to be done. But sometimes organization isn't what's important. Sometimes sitting on the couch with a mug of tea, a blanket, and a good book is the better way to spend an evening.

Her dark hair hangs loose around her shoulders and a tendril keeps falling forward. She reaches up to tuck it behind her ear, and adjusts her glasses. Her blue eyes sparkle in the low light and her lips part in a smile. I'd love to know what's going through her mind—what caused that flicker of happiness to cross her features.

Is it too much to hope that it was thoughts of me?

She tucks her feet under her favorite blanket to warm them. I almost get up and find her a pair of socks. But I'm rooted to the spot, watching her from the corner of my eye. She's a bit like a wild animal in the forest. I'm seeing a glimpse of her in her natural environment, and I don't want to ruin the moment.

It's even better that her natural environment is here, with me.

Time has passed, and we've discovered all the things about each other that can drive the wrong person away. We know each other's annoying habits. Likes and dislikes. I know she hates crowds and loud commercials. She likes too much salt on her food and hates cheesecake. She knows I take long showers and leave the cap off the toothpaste. How I like to cook but hate grocery shopping.

But our quirks and idiosyncrasies fit together, as smooth as chocolate sauce poured over ice cream.

She fills a hole inside me that I hadn't realized was empty. Before her, my life wasn't bad. I told myself I didn't need anything else. But since she crashed into my life—because *crashed* is exactly how it happened—I've been fulfilled in a way I never imagined was possible.

I've written more than a dozen happily ever afters. Until her, I thought they were a fantasy. But the truth is, she *is* the happily ever after.

She's like the best book ever written. I want to run my fingers down her spine. I want to turn her pages and read her truth, savoring every word. I want to be the one who gets to read the secret parts, the chapters she only shows with great trust. And when I'm finished, I won't shelve her. I won't put her back with the rest to collect dust, while the memory of her words fade. Not only do I want to read her over and over again, I want to help her write the rest.

I want to co-star in the ending.

. . .

I LOOK up from my Kindle and gasp. Alex is standing right next to me. I was so caught up in what I was reading, I didn't realize he came over.

His eyes hold mine and he lowers himself down onto one knee.

"What are you doing?" I ask.

"Shh," he says. "You're not supposed to talk yet."

I press my lips together. My heart beats hard and a flutter of nerves tingles my belly.

I want to co-star in the ending.

"I love you," he says. "And I want to be the last man who ever gets to love you." He lifts his hand. Pinched between his finger and thumb is a gold band with a row of inset diamonds. "Mia, will you marry me?"

"Oh... I mean... a ring... I mean..." I stop and close my eyes, taking a deep breath to center myself. "Yes."

"Yes?" he asks.

"Of course," I say with a laugh. "Did you think I'd say no?"

He smiles and I melt into a puddle of happiness. He takes my hand and slips the ring onto my finger.

"Oh my god, Alex, we're engaged?" I throw my arms around his neck, nearly knocking him over. He laughs and hugs me back, his arms so strong. He keeps me safe and steady.

He pulls back and touches my cheek, his hand warm against my skin. His eyes are deep and fierce. He leans in and claims my mouth with his, kissing me with passion and intensity. I surrender to him, letting him take me. I'm his and I always will be.

He gets on the couch and pulls me into his lap, kissing me again. I always wondered if I'd ever find someone who would love me the way I am—awkward quirks and all. I thought men like Alex only existed on the pages of my favorite books.

But here he is, holding me. Kissing me. Loving me. Better than any book boyfriend I've ever read.

He's mine, and I'm his. Neither of us are perfect, but we're perfect for each other.

And that's what they mean when they say, *and they lived happily ever after*.

DEAR READER

Dear reader,

First off, the answer to a question at least a few of you are asking right about now. Who are YOU, really?

Is this my story? Am I a guy like Alex, who found unexpected success writing romance under a female pen name? Is this the book I wrote to apologize to the woman I love for lying to her?

Nope. I'm really a girl.

It's a great idea though, isn't it?

Actually, this idea came from my husband, who many of you know as Mr. Arm Porn. Mr. AP turned to me one night, out of the blue, and said, "What if you wrote a book about a guy who is a writer, and he starts writing romance with a female pen name. And what if he met a girl and she didn't know who he was, but he knew who she was. That might be good."

And I said something like, "You mad genius, I have to write that!"

So I did.

It wasn't that easy though. This book tested me. There were nights when I stared at the screen, wondering if I was going to be able to pull this off. This book is the result of a lot of hard work, and a lot of MUCH appreciated brainstorming help from several people (Tammi, Nikki, and Mr. AP, I'm looking at you).

I was faced with writing a hero who is admittedly lying to the heroine for a good portion of the book. How do you deal with that? How do you make that a) believable, and b) forgive-able. Yes, I realize some of you were probably pulling your hair out, thinking of other solutions for Alex that didn't involve lies. Many of you probably caught on to the fact that Mia wasn't a stranger to him, so he could have trusted her from the start.

But here's the thing about Alex. He's divorced. His dad is divorced. His mom is fairly absent. His brother lost his wife. His sister is struggling to find love. He doesn't see *forever* when he looks at anyone. He sees temporary.

That's not because he's a jerk or wants to use women or man-whore his way through life. He's just not so sure happily-ever-after is a real thing that people can hope for. So when he's faced with the truth about Mia—that she's his good friend BB—he doesn't think he can risk telling her the truth. And he's a decent enough guy that he doesn't want to try to be two people with her.

That is, until he sees her again, of course. She's too much. Everything about her is appealing to him. He can't stay away.

Mia is one of my favorite heroines to date. She's a little awkward, a little quirky (as my heroines often are), and a lot of fun. She's used to people thinking she's a little odd, and she's happy with who she is. But she'd sure like to find some of that love she keeps reading about. She's just not sure men like the ones in books exist.

I think we all wonder that sometimes.

From the beginning, I wanted to be very meta with this book. It begins at the crisis in their relationship—not a typical place to begin a story. The book Alex writes to Mia begins in the same way, as if that's the very book you're reading. In fact, it bears the same name.

I also sprinkled in romance reader culture references throughout the book—things voracious romance readers will be familiar with. Even the title, Book Boyfriend, is a homage to romance readers everywhere, who love their book boyfriends.

I hope Alex was a book boyfriend you can swoon over. He was a very enjoyable character to write, as was Mia. I hope you had as much fun with them as I did.

Thanks for reading!

CK

ALSO BY CLAIRE KINGSLEY

For a full and up-to-date listing of Claire Kingsley books visit www.clairekingsleybooks.com/books/

For comprehensive reading order, visit www.clairekingsleybooks.com/reading-order/

The Haven Brothers

Small-town romantic suspense with CK's signature endearing characters and heartwarming happily ever afters. Can be read as stand-alones.

Obsession Falls (Josiah and Audrey)

Storms and Secrets (Zachary and Marigold)

The rest of the Haven brothers will be getting their own happily ever afters!

How the Grump Saved Christmas (Elias and Isabelle)

A stand-alone, small-town Christmas romance.

The Bailey Brothers

Steamy, small-town family series with a dash of suspense. Five unruly brothers. Epic pranks. A quirky, feuding town. Big HEAs. Best read in order.

Protecting You (Asher and Grace part 1)

Fighting for Us (Asher and Grace part 2)

Unraveling Him (Evan and Fiona)

Rushing In (Gavin and Skylar)

Chasing Her Fire (Logan and Cara)

Rewriting the Stars (Levi and Annika)

~

The Miles Family

Sexy, sweet, funny, and heartfelt family series with a dash of suspense.
Messy family. Epic bromance. Super romantic. Best read in order.

Broken Miles (Roland and Zoe)

Forbidden Miles (Brynn and Chase)

Reckless Miles (Cooper and Amelia)

Hidden Miles (Leo and Hannah)

Gaining Miles: A Miles Family Novella (Ben and Shannon)

~

Dirty Martini Running Club

Sexy, fun, feel-good romantic comedies with huge... hearts. Can be
read as stand-alones.

Everly Dalton's Dating Disasters (Prequel with Everly, Hazel, and Nora)

Faking Ms. Right (Everly and Shepherd)

Falling for My Enemy (Hazel and Corban)

Marrying Mr. Wrong (Sophie and Cox)

Flirting with Forever (Nora and Dex)

Bluewater Billionaires

Hot romantic comedies. Lady billionaire BFFs and the badass heroes who love them. Can be read as stand-alones.

The Mogul and the Muscle (Cameron and Jude)

The Price of Scandal, Wild Open Hearts, and Crazy for Loving You

More Bluewater Billionaire shared-world romantic comedies by Lucy Score, Kathryn Nolan, and Pippa Grant

Bootleg Springs

by Claire Kingsley and Lucy Score

Hot and hilarious small-town romcom series with a dash of mystery and suspense. Best read in order.

Whiskey Chaser (Scarlett and Devlin)

Sidecar Crush (Jameson and Leah Mae)

Moonshine Kiss (Bowie and Cassidy)

Bourbon Bliss (June and George)

Gin Fling (Jonah and Shelby)

Highball Rush (Gibson and I can't tell you)

Book Boyfriends

Hot romcoms that will make you laugh and make you swoon. Can be read as stand-alones.

Book Boyfriend (Alex and Mia)

Cocky Roommate (Weston and Kendra)

Hot Single Dad (Caleb and Linnea)

Finding Ivy (William and Ivy)

A unique contemporary romance with a hint of mystery. Stand-alone.

His Heart (Sebastian and Brooke)

A poignant and emotionally intense story about grief, loss, and the transcendent power of love. Stand-alone.

The Always Series

Smoking hot, dirty talking bad boys with some angsty intensity. Can be read as stand-alones.

Always Have (Braxton and Kylie)

Always Will (Selene and Ronan)

Always Ever After (Braxton and Kylie)

The Jetty Beach Series

Sexy small-town romance series with swoony heroes, romantic HEAs, and lots of big feels. Can be read as stand-alones.

Behind His Eyes (Ryan and Nicole)

One Crazy Week (Melissa and Jackson)

Messy Perfect Love (Cody and Clover)

Operation Get Her Back (Hunter and Emma)

ABOUT THE AUTHOR

Claire Kingsley is a #1 Amazon bestselling author of sexy, heartfelt contemporary romance and romantic comedies. She writes sassy, quirky heroines, swoony heroes who love their women hard, panty-melting sexytimes, romantic happily ever afters, and all the big feels.

She can't imagine life without coffee, her Kindle, and the sexy heroes who inhabit her imagination. She lives in the inland Pacific Northwest with her three kids.

www.clairekingsleybooks.com